STORIES

TÉA MUTONJI

AN IMPRINT OF ARSENAL PULP PRESS
VANCOUVER

SHUT UP YOU'RE PRETTY

FIFTH PRINTING: 2024

VS. BOOKS
An imprint of
ARSENAL PULP PRESS
Suite 202 – 211 East Georgia St.
Vancouver, BC V6A 1Z6
Canada
arsenalpulp.com
vsbooks.ca

The publisher gratefully acknowledges the support of the Canada Council for the Arts and the British Columbia Arts Council for its publishing program, and the Government of Canada, and the Government of British Columbia (through the Book Publishing Tax Credit Program), for its publishing activities.

Arsenal Pulp Press acknowledges the xʷməθkʷəy̓əm (Musqueam), Sḵwx̱wú7mesh (Squamish), and səl̓ilwətaʔɬ (Tsleil-Waututh) Nations, speakers of Hul'q'umi'num'/Halq'eméylem/hən̓q̓əmin̓əm̓ən̓q custodians of the traditional, ancestral, and unceded territories where our office is located. We pay respect to their histories, traditions, and continuous living cultures and commit to accountability, respectful relations, and friendship.

This is a work of fiction. Any resemblance of characters to persons either living or deceased is purely coincidental.

Cover and text design by Oliver McPartlin
Edited by Vivek Shraya
Copy edited by Shirarose Wilensky
Proofread by Doretta Lau

Printed and bound in Canada

Library and Archives Canada Cataloguing in Publication:

Mutonji, Téa, 1994–, author

Shut up, you're pretty / Téa Mutonji.
Short stories.
Issued in print and electronic formats.
ISBN 978-1-55152-755-0 (softcover).—ISBN 978-1-55152-756-7 (HTML)
I. Title. II. Title: Shut up, you are pretty.
PS8626.U92S58 2019 C813'.6 C2018-906218-5
C2018-906219-3

To my sisters, Maïta and Ornella

CONTENTS

TITS FOR CIGS

Jolie was my first friend. Her name was actually Jolietta. I shortened it to Jolie upon meeting her. I felt it captured her spirit more, her essence. The name came from a song Mother used to sing when we lived in Congo, where it was hot and mosquitoes didn't sting because we coexisted with them. "Mommy's baby, pretty, pretty," the song went. Mother stopped singing once we immigrated. She stopped doing many things. But I liked that she had given me this—this song so that I could now give it to someone else. And Jolie was in fact *jolie*: long blonde hair, defined nose, blue in her eyes, roses in each cheek, tall but not defiantly so.

She was the one who introduced me to the park. She was responsible for my popularity and my likability, because she was herself popular and well liked, and I gained her reputation by proximity. But still, I was the girl next door. Unlike Jolie, I had perfectly ashy elbows and naturally lacked poise, and this was my advantage on Galloway. People could relate to that. As for Jolie, she was simply unattainable. To want a person like her was to want too much from life. To have a person like her was to have everything and, perhaps, too soon.

When we arrived, Jolie was sitting on our doorstep, as though to check that the newcomers weren't freaks. And then she gave a thumbs-up to a bunch of kids watching from the other side of the roundabout. There was another set of low-rise townhomes, peeling and brown, identical to ours. The thumbs-up meant that we were acceptable, that we had passed some unknown street cred test, and Jolie was both curator and writer of said test.

She introduced herself as we were unloading the suitcases from the taxi. That's all we had. Suitcases. We were lucky enough that the previous tenants had left behind some furniture and that whoever ran the complex took pity on our poverty and allowed us to claim it as our own.

"Welcome to Galloway," Jolie said, reaching her hand out to greet my father. As they shook hands, she grimaced a smile at him, stuck her tongue out, and winked. "Can he come out and play?" she asked.

We all looked at Junior.

"Not him," Jolie said. "The other one."

"Loli?" my father said, and that's when we all realized she was referring to me.

"Is she a girl or a boy?" Jolie tilted her head.

My English was still just so-so, but this I understood. It had become a frequent question, though my hair had grown significantly since we landed. Before we left, I was given a buzz cut to match the picture of the boy in the passport I had used to come here. Nobody thought that it would work. I looked too feminine: too soft—soft nose, soft eyes, soft mouth, soft ears, soft cheeks. But by the time we got to the security gate at the airport, the soldiers were distracted, and nobody questioned me. But for a week after we arrived in Canada, I copied the way my brother walked, the way he ate, yawned, and brushed his teeth. Nobody told me when it was safe to stop pretending, and I found that I enjoyed this very much. I seemed to be more liked. More respected. But it might have been that people who knew what we had to do as refugees pitied me. So they showered me with gifts and compliments as though any of those things could confirm anyone's sex. But I wasn't confused. I knew who I was. I just found Junior's jeans more comfortable. And his shoes made more sense. So I never quite stopped dressing like him. I played video games. And for as long as I could, I kept my hair short.

Maybe it was her age. Maybe it was the season. But Jolie was the only person to actually confuse me. But she was also the only person who believed me when I said, "I'm not sad—not even a little bit."

"Where are your parents?" my father asked her.

"Around," Jolie said. "Probably locked up in unit 86. It's on the south side of the complex. In front of the park. If you want to come meet my mom."

"You pray?" my father said.

"To God, you mean?" Jolie said, then she slapped her palm on her forehead. "Obviously."

"Good," my father said.

It was decided.

Mother, my brother, and my father went inside our unit, and I followed Jolie.

On our walk to the park, she told me that the number one rule of the street was to tell men exactly what they wanted to hear.

"Usually," she told me. "Sometimes, though, it turns them on to hear no."

I followed Jolie silently, and we walked slowly. Every few units, a kid would be standing on their porch—which was really just part of the sidewalk that led to their unit—and they'd stare as we walked by. I got the impression of Jolie right then and there: a showstopper, a credible figure in this neighbourhood, perhaps royalty. She talked and talked and talked. Mostly about the neighbourhood. The boundaries and the places to avoid. She talked about her mother, Gigi, who was a nurse but was currently unemployed. As she went on, all I could think of was that song.

"Jolie," I said. "Do people ever call you Jolie?"

So the name stuck. And I was so proud to have been the one to give it to her.

Jolie was wearing a jean skirt and tank top that had been cut to reveal her midriff. She had fuchsia on her lips and her hair in a high side ponytail. She was a strange mixture between child and angel, the kind you saw in religious picture books, designed to inspire hope in you. But she also had that rag-doll look that made her one of us—hard, used, and tired.

"Do you have any cigarettes?" she asked.

We were stopped at the intersection of Lawrence and Galloway. You got the best of Scarborough exactly here: the low-income houses attached to the getting-by houses, attached to the getting-there houses. But something felt so telling and obvious about this exact intersection. I had the sense that my life was changing, far more than it already had.

Jolie had a very good walk. Later, I told my mom that when we were older, Jolie would be a model, and I would be her personal assistant. Mom said I could be a model too, if I wanted, but Jolie said, "Braids aren't allowed on the runway," before pushing them behind my ears.

"We're going to need cigarettes," she announced. "Or else I'll die!"

Jolie was glistening. Her hair, her mouth, the way she said "cigarettes."

We went to the convenience store. It was a family business, though we only ever saw one of the two sons working the register. There was the gay one, Cory, and the one who refused to give us his name. The nameless one was older, and, once, we caught him masturbating to the women in the magazines. Forever after, we could expect free stuff. Neither of them could have been over eighteen, but to us they were so old. Every future trip to the store was made after long hours of fixing our hair and lowering our shirts to show our cleavage. I was chubby in comparison to Jolie, but she explained to me that it was just baby fat. She'd wrap an elastic right underneath my breasts to bring them together. But every guy who talked to me did so to get closer to her. In retrospect, I was in the best position ever.

Jolie told me that I had to arch my back. "So that your boobies are up." Then, taking one good look at me, she said, "Are you wearing anything underneath that?" She was referring to my shirt printed with a huge picture of Tupac. I had a tank top underneath, which Jolie tied behind my back, saying, "Perfect—you're perfect!"

"I have a plan," she told me. "Do you trust me?"

I mean, I had just met her. All I knew so far was that she was fearless. She was so involved with life as both a concept and a chore. She was different from anyone I had ever met.

"Yes," I told her.

"Good," she said, and grabbed my face, kissed me on my forehead.

The first guy walked past us completely. He was wearing a sweater and ripped jeans before they became a thing.

The next guy said, "How old are you guys anyway?"

"We're not guys," Jolie said. "We're basically women."

The guy after that laughed and bought us lollipops instead. Jolie took the candies and laughed so hard the building behind us seem to shake. I wasn't entirely sure what was so funny, but I laughed too.

The guy after that was short and stubby, with tomato hair. He had a button-up shirt and good pants, pimples around his mouth.

"Tits for cigs," Jolie shouted.

"Excuse me?" the man said.

"I'll show you my boobs if you buy us cigarettes."

The man adjusted his shirt. "What about her?" he said.

"She'll let you touch them."

The man disappeared inside the store without another word. We stood silently, trying not to make eye contact, watching the cars drive by, certain they knew what we were doing, that life was coming and we weren't trying to stop it.

After a while, the man came back, cigarettes in hand.

"Drop the cigarettes," Jolie said with a shaking voice that made it sound more like "op duh si-ga-rette."

"Shouldn't you girls be in school?"

"We don't have school," I said, in case he thought I was the assistant.

"All right, a deal's a deal," he said, leading us behind the building. He moved in closer to me until my back was pinned against the wall.

"The cigarettes!" Jolie said, with so much bravado I wondered if the frustration came from the way he looked at me and not at her. I felt very attached to the smell of his breath: coffee and old age confined together.

"The cigarettes," I said, while lifting my shirt and giving him a good look. With one hand, he slid the pack inside mine; with the other, he took a handful of fat and squeezed.

"There you go, that's right," I said, imagining myself to be one of the girls in the porn magazines. I had forgotten Jolie's small body behind him until she repeated, "There you go, that's right," so slowly a year went over my head.

The moment ended when Jolie grabbed the cigarettes and yanked me away. We ran as fast as we could, threw ourselves on the empty field behind the housing complex.

"What did I tell you?" Jolie said, lighting her cigarette. "We are women!"

I laughed so hard, as hard as she did, feeling the grass shaking.

"Who are we?" Jolie shouted.

"Women!"

"What do we want?"

"Cigarettes!"

Jolie took off her shirt as if she was born to be shirtless, the daylight landing on her chest, the wind, the trees, the entire world cheering as she got up and ran in circles, her breasts moving like homemade Jell-O.

PARCHMENT PAPER

I met my cousin Theresa several months after my family moved to Galloway. I was well acquainted with the neighbourhood by then. Had made friends. Had people who knew me by name and would knock on the door and ask for me. Had grown my hair. I felt quite secure with myself and my status among my peers. But then Theresa came to visit that summer.

She was the kind of kid you didn't want to argue with. She was raised by a doctor and a successful artist and believed this gave her some rights. She was all height, no hips, flat chest, and a pinched-in stomach. She was strong, and she moved wisely, walked with a dance that never went unnoticed. She was shoulders pulled apart from each other, a warm smile, skin like water.

I woke up one day and she was in my bed.

"Who are you?" I said.

"Don't just lie around and stare at me! Can I get some water?"

It was an odd response considering she was in my bed, and she had been the one watching me sleep. I accepted it anyway, as a defence mechanism. I went down to the kitchen and poured her a glass from the tap. We were alone in the house—my brother, Junior, out playing some sport, Mother working at one of her many jobs, and my father doing what he called "Man's Work."

Theresa was in a yellow polka-dot dress when I went back up. She drank her water slowly, her pinky sticking out. She did this to establish dominance. To state the obvious hierarchy between us. And I loved her for it. It was classy and honest. She wouldn't tell me how she came to be in my bed or how long she would be staying, and I knew better than to ask Mother later because such questioning of her authority might result in a spanking. There was a bright orange suitcase on the floor. And the vanity was now dressed with oils, hair products, and elastics.

Theresa rose from the bed and walked her fingers along the walls of my bedroom. They were yellow from the previous tenant with a splash of pink on the ceiling. People weren't supposed to modify government housing, but the previous tenant had replaced the carpet and every single screen door. These were things Theresa wouldn't know how to appreciate. Instead, she dug her nail into the wall, scraped some of it off.

"It's fake," she said.

"It's wallpaper," I said.

"What's that smell? So offensive. What is it?"

Theresa was older by two years and had an extensive vocabulary. She went on to tell me that her house was built with hallways, windows, and hidden closets. That my house was "cute" in comparison. There were no further details about her life. I followed her around asking, desperate to fill the space in my mind that was reserved for people like her: grand, larger-than-life, spirited.

It took Theresa two weeks to become integrated with us. Once she got over the smallness of where we lived, she seemed to fit right in. She told me that my family was poor, as an explanation for the lack of food and air conditioning in the house. She told me that poverty was like cancer, that there was no cure, but that I could live a fine life anyway.

I enjoyed showing her around Galloway. We were complete opposites but got along well, with that soft innocence of childhood stupidity: dolls, roses, Hula-Hoops. With most of my friends, I wanted to age. I wanted to have grey hair and a person to drink wine with. And with my brother, I wanted to low-ride my jeans and play on every single team. It was different with Theresa. I wanted to rely on my impulses, my inner gut feeling. She was so good at that.

"Do you know what people call me?" she asked.

"Tess? Tessa?"

“Tree Legs.”

“Tree Legs,” I repeated.

“Because I have long legs,” she said. “Boys are always trying to climb up my tree legs. You'll understand by the time you get to be my age.”

In the days that followed, Theresa wore a series of summer dresses. Pastel colours. Short, exposing her coconut knees. And on the afternoons we planned to watch Junior play basketball, she'd stuff the sweetheart neckline with socks or scrunched-up newspaper.

I leaned my head on her shoulder, while we sat on the sidelines, cheering.

“How old where you when you had your first kiss?” I said.

“Old, and it was online. Why?”

“Like, on webcam?”

“We just kissed through the screen. I learned everything on the internet.”

“With tongue?”

“Of course with tongue. We were obviously just licking the screen, but something about it made us feel very connected.” Theresa brought two fingers to her mouth and stuck her tongue in between them.

“That's really cool,” I said.

She moved her body so that my head slipped from its support.

That was the summer Theresa became obsessed with the word “cunt.” On any given night, she might come home and claim she had been followed. “He called me a cunt!” she'd shout, while changing into her nightgown. “Can you believe it? A cunt!”

Theresa would open her mouth wide, holding the flashlight like a gun. “What do you think snatch means?”

I didn't know, and usually, whenever we hit a brick wall like this, we would move on to a new activity.

Later, in bed, she'd tell me, “I was just kidding about the men.” To which I'd say, “I know.”

Theresa was exactly who I wanted to be when I grew up. She had an answer for every question, an explanation for every argument, a how-to guide for every problem. We once saw a man at the intersection of Galloway and Lawrence with a small teardrop tattoo. It meant he had killed someone, Theresa told me, and lost the love of his life because of it. Detailed, I thought. Didn't understand how she could get all of that from a tattoo.

"Excuse me, sir," she said. "I just wanted to say that I'm sorry for your loss. I'm sure you'll find somebody else!"

The man surprised us both when he leaned in and kissed her on the forehead.

It was the first week of August. I liked this part of the summer. It was the limbo. We had exhausted our imaginations, had played every single street game, sport, and exercise. All we could do now was fill our days with repetition.

Every day, Theresa and I woke up to each other and wrote a list of things we needed to do. But on this day it was so hot Theresa declared we do only one thing. Usually our day involved a few hours at a swimming pool in the area. And if we couldn't get access to a building, then Theresa would suggest we get creative. Either by running through sprinklers or shooting each other with hoses. But on this day Theresa suggested we fill the tub with water.

"It's your parents," she said. "They aren't paying the bills again."

She said "again" as if we'd known each other for years.

In the bathroom, I watched Theresa fill the tub to the brim. Her body seemed to shrink behind the fabric of her dress. She ran her arms through the water, occasionally looking back at me, as if this was the most radical idea and she the most radical person. She undressed, and I felt a strange sensation. A shiver. Like a cold wind had quickly passed through me.

I had never seen a real person fully naked, in the flesh. In pictures, yes. Often, my best friend Jolie and I might find magazines and flip through them to touch the women wherever we wanted. But I had never been this close. I took off my shirt, jumped out of my jeans, and walked over. Then, once I was before her, I took off my underwear.

"Shut up," she said, pointing at my body. "You've got a bush."

I stood there, not entirely sure whether to conceal myself or get in the tub.

"I can fix that for you," she said. "I know this amazing wax recipe from the internet."

"Wax what?"

"Your bush," she said. "I can wax your bush. You won't even feel a thing."

Theresa caressed her body on the cold surface of the water. I could see her right nipple poking outside of her crossed arms.

We went downstairs. I was still naked, but Theresa was wrapped in a towel. Theresa arranged me on the kitchen floor. In my periphery, I watched her boil white glue, chicken broth, and a pinch of salt in a pot. That's when she started to open up to me, as though stirring the recipe calmed her down. I didn't even need to ask. All I had to do was lie still.

Theresa crouched down next to me and scooped the paste over my pubic hair, then pressed a piece of parchment paper over the wax. It was hot and thick and dried instantly. She talked and talked and talked throughout. She told me how her mother had lost all her beauty crying over the divorce. She offered this so casually, as though still referring to pubic hair, massaging the parchment paper and stopping only to blow air in between my legs. I don't know when I stopped listening to her and started focusing on the sensation inside of me.

Then she gasped, "Fuck," and my eyes blinked open.

"Shit, fuck, shit, fuck." Her eyes looked directly into mine. "Do you feel anything?"

I looked down. The piece of parchment paper had attached itself to me like a second layer of skin.

"I don't know what to do," she said.

"It's not coming off?"

"You don't feel it when I try to pull? I don't know."

"Try again!"

Theresa tried, but the paper stayed put. I waited for her to say that it wasn't her fault, that the paper was cheap, that I had let the hair grow too long and there was no way around it.

"I'm gonna get a knife," Theresa said instead.

She instructed me to cover my eyes, and I stupidly listened to her. I could feel a hard, cold, flat stick scraping along the edge of the paper. Theresa was going slowly, so slowly, I slipped away again, and focused only on the feeling.

Then, there was a stab inside of me. A long and piercing pain that seemed to follow a straight line. And then it felt good.

I could feel Theresa panic and the quick movement of her arms pivoting around me. And then, as I tried to sit up, the knife just glided right out of me.

There was a moment of silence. Theresa looked away. And then I looked away. And we sat there on the kitchen floor, a wet knife between us.

"Maybe you should go back in the tub," she said after a while. "Maybe the water will loosen the paper."

I didn't object. I went up and sat in the tub alone. I rocked my body in a circular motion.

For a week after, I felt exhausted and hot and locked myself in my bedroom. I was desperate to feel that way again. I would reach for a toothbrush or a hairbrush, a pencil, a pen, anything, really. I didn't know what this meant, and I didn't care. I loved the feeling. I loved the way my stomach did somersaults whenever I found myself alone. I would spend hours masturbating, never tiring. I wouldn't answer if anyone came to the door. I wouldn't go out anywhere with Theresa. And from my bedroom window, I could hear that Theresa had replaced me. I could hear Theresa and this new me playing in the backyard. And when they called for me, I would throw my pillow over my head and wait until the calling was over.

I didn't get to say goodbye to Theresa before she left. She went the exact same way she came. In the middle of the night and without a word.

THE EVENT

My best friend Jolie and I spent every evening after school in the park. It was an abandoned soccer field behind our housing complex that nearly got turned into a cemetery. It was where gang members used to host meetings or throw parties—which looked exactly same. But the park was also a place of serenity. It sat across from the main road, tucked behind a row of mature trees. Green instead of salmon, like the brick of our units. A wall between us and them.

We were the kids of Galloway and they were anyone who judged us for it.

Jolie and I sat on the ground and held our breath, eyes closed, lips pressed together. The one who could hold off the longest won. But there was no prize and no other rules. In fact, there was barely a game. It didn't have an end goal. There was just the two of us and the park. Somewhere to go. Somewhere to run away. We lay together.

"Do you know that people smoke cigarettes to cure anxiety?" Jolie said.

"Is what you have now?"

"I'm just saying."

"Are you really going to get a job?" I asked.

"Don't listen to that whore mouth Gigi."

"Well, I have a plan."

"Does it involve working to fulfil one of Gigi's conspiracy theories?"

"That depends," I said. "Would you say kissing is work?"

Jolie sat up straight. She crossed her arms in front of her chest. "You do realize that my mother, the woman you adore so much, is a druggie, right?"

It was true that I had a fascination with Gigi. She was a first edition of Jolie. More accessible. More easy. Her addiction gave her magnitude and charm, and a good base for redemption. But more than that, Gigi was the most beautiful woman I had ever seen. The heroin had only tired her out. Darkened her teeth and brightened her hair. She would hide the bruises on her skin, so in public it was easy to mistake her for someone who simply had a rough night out.

Jolie graced the contours of my knee with her fingers, and then stretched back down. The long drape of her hair meshed with the grass.

"Do you remember how Dylan paid us to kiss last week?"

"I remember his baby boner, yes."

"What do you think?"

"He's not my type."

"He paid us."

"Yes, he did, I remember."

It took Jolie a moment to hear me out, but once she did, her face lit up.

It was getting late, and it was too cold to sleep outside. I took Jolie's hand and led the way back to my house. Gigi had recently gotten back together with Steve, and Jolie couldn't go home when he was around. He made it very clear he didn't like children, though of course he'd never touch a hair on Jolie's head. The beatings were reserved for Gigi, and we did our best not to be around to witness them. If we did, Gigi would laugh and change her scream to sound like a moan. Later, she'd declare, "Ladies, best advice I can give you, be wary of men who know what they're doing in the bedroom. They'll destroy every part of you, if you know what I mean." Then Gigi would look for Advil, but that was part of the show. She was really looking for a baggie or a needle.

Now that Jolie was turning fourteen, Gigi had gotten it into her head that she needed to help with rent. We lived in a subsidized neighbourhood and rent was mostly reasonable. The ones who couldn't afford it might have a two-month grace period before the locks were changed and police started coming around the entire block. We collectively tried to prevent the latter from happening. It wasn't uncommon for Mrs Broomfield to go door to door with a basket asking for money to help somebody in need. But nobody looked after Gigi anymore. It was just Jolie. It was just Jolie and me.

Gigi had a friend with a catering company who had agreed to hire Jolie under the table. But we didn't trust Gigi.

In the morning, we went out to find Dylan. We told him an event was taking place at the park. With a silent nod, we all knew what the event would be. Dylan had a very sober face, earnest and strong. And behind the dark circles under his eyes, I saw a little boy dreaming of a Jamaican waterfront. Dylan was sweet, sugar-coated.

In the evening, Jolie and I wore matching crop tops and sat facing each other at the park. There were three boys with Dylan, and we charged them each five dollars. The night went by quickly. Nobody asked for an encore. Nobody clapped or cheered or growled like we had expected. Everybody went on their own personal journey, and the intimacy was felt in a gaze. Jolie looking at me, me looking at Jolie, them looking at us.

The next day there were five of them. And on Friday there were six. That was a total of seventy-five dollars by the end our first week. I loved Jolie. I loved her so much I told her to keep the money.

"Are you sure about this?" she asked, bringing the money to her nostrils. "This is what Gigi does," she said, sniffing the money.

I was sure.

Jolie gave some of the money to Gigi, but we used most of it to buy cigarettes, treats, cosmetics. The park still belonged to us. Even though we shared it. Outside of business hours people seemed to know that it belonged to us. There was peace there. Nothing else.

"We should flash them," I said. "Charge five dollars for a kiss, and ten for anything more."

"Fifteen for a kiss, a flash, and a three-way."

"Like we kiss, and then we kiss them?"

"It has to be step by step. We kiss each other, then we flash them, and then they kiss us."

"We should charge more for that. Twenty, at least."

"Twenty-five with tongue."

The event was a hit. Our days suddenly felt anticlimactic, as every night we were putting on a show. Afterwards, Jolie and I would just read. And be together.

I got the best of Jolie in the afternoons. She'd be happy and singing, and I'd shape my body into a starfish, enjoying her happiness. She was a good dancer too. And she had a voice on her. She would sing a mix of popular love songs while I read, and then she would run her fingers down my back, and back up.

It was a weekend and it hadn't snowed yet and we were enjoying the simplicity. The park would have been empty if not for us. But the shadows of the housing complex felt like company. We could see Mrs Broomfield behind the fence that led to the south block sweeping leaves in her backyard. Next door, Darnell's silhouette seemed to be stroking guitar strings in the dimness of the kitchen light. And outside, though we couldn't see them, we heard younger girls laughing.

Jolie pushed my braids behind my ear. "I like this look on you." She was referring to my hair, but I got the feeling there was more to it. For the first time, she kissed me because she wanted to. Her real and unrehearsed lips were warm and soft and unlike anything I could have imagined.

Two months went by and we could expect ten to twelve boys per night. Jolie told me she gave a blow job to a college guy as a way to get close to him and others like him. Her plan worked. We were a hit with college boys.

But we found that working every day took away our credibility. Jolie argued that it made us seem too desperate and readily available. So, instead, the event was held only on Thursdays. We could expect fifteen to twenty guys on any given Thursday. Never any girls. They all stopped talking to us once the money really started coming in. But we were swimming in it, and we couldn't stop.

One night, it was just Dylan and me.

"Do you want to touch me?" I asked. "You don't have to pay me."

"You're a really sweet girl," he began, and I could hear the etcetera,

etcetera, etcetera, so I leaned forward and kissed him. Kissed him like I had been kissing Jolie but with less consciousness. It lasted a minute. Maybe even less than that.

Dylan pulled away. "You're like a sister to me—you know that."

I did. I also knew that the crowd wasn't coming in to see two girls kissing but to see Jolie being kissed.

Dylan stopped coming to the event on Thursdays.

Jolie bought us matching winter jackets. Black with Baby Phat written in gold cursive on the right arm.

"So I guess Steve's moving in for real for real."

"Good old Stevie boy," I said.

"I'll basically have to fuck him to get rid of him now."

"Yeah, basically."

We had our largest crowd late in November, just before the snow took over. Twenty-two boys. None of whom I recognized. All of whom seemed to be familiar with Jolie.

Jolie and I faced each other. We kissed. Slow and steady.

"With tongue," I heard someone say.

I turned to the crowd. "That's an extra two dollars," I insisted.

Somebody threw a toonie at us. I poked my tongue inside Jolie's mouth and she giggled.

"Twenty dollars if you finger her!"

Jolie laughed, which was good. I hadn't heard her laugh since Steve moved in. She pinned me to the ground and got on top of me. The last thing I remember: she grabbed a bouquet of her hair and tied it with her bracelet.

Then we smoked cigarettes on the damp grass. It hadn't rained or anything. The earth was just getting ready for winter.

"We're porn stars," I said.

"More than that. We're *real* stars," Jolie said.

We went Christmas shopping at the Morningside Mall. Even though we had the money, we stole something from every store. For the thrill. We tried on wigs and cowboy hats and heard from the woman at guest services that the mall would be shutting down. We had a funeral: rest in peace sweet escalators, rest in peace Victoria's Secret, rest in peace Hot Dog man.

Jolie turned fourteen in January. I left the window open in case she needed a place to sleep. Her fingers were burning hot when she got in bed. They wrapped around my waist and met at the centre of my stomach.

"Are you awake?"

"I'm dead. I'm dying."

She was hot. And whispery. And sweating. "I did a thing."

I waited to hear about the thing.

"I fucked Steve."

Jolie kissed my neck. I kept my eyes closed. So I could wake up and decide which part happened and which part I imagined.

"Was it your first time?" I said.

"Well. Sort of. I mean, once with Dylan."

I turned to face her. In her eyes, I saw that little boy again—drowning in the ocean. Dylan and Jolie. I couldn't picture it.

DOWN THE LAKESHORE

It was true what they said about my father. He was a dreamer. He was a poet in his mannerisms. In his own personal torture. All intense and empty eyes. The contradictions could make you uncomfortable. But even when I first met him, after Mother, Junior, and I immigrated to Canada from Congo, I knew he was my father. I was six years old, but I knew. It was like hearing my own heartbeat.

My father was light brown. It was a commodity back in Congo. He looked like he might have had some white in him, and since his mother, the original woman, was accused of fucking around, people talked all they wanted. Junior and I were so dark, but people never questioned whether we were his children. People only talked about Mother. She was a purebred. Mbulas in every way. Ate spices and prayed twice a day. Hard-working. Strong features.

My father would typically be gone in the morning when I woke and wouldn't make it home in time for dinner. The longest I went living underneath the same roof without once seeing him was two months. It was better in the summer. I would wake up extra early to send him off.

Most mornings, I felt as though he needed a second to remember who I was. I'd wave my hand and say, "Hello, it's me? The daughter you abandoned? You know? The only one."

He took such remarks well. He would lean forward and say, "How do *you* know you're the only one."

We tried the whole coy-humour thing as a way to ignore the pain. It worked well. For years I believed my father was a happy man.

Sometimes he'd pick me up from school and we'd walk to the Go train station. He insisted on sitting near the window, opposite from me. This he did every single time. These trips were the only times we spent together.

It was winter, which meant he wasn't needed at his second job. I didn't know what the second job was. I just knew he had to commute for hours to get there. And despite it being winter, he still insisted on wearing a suit, a tie, dress pants. No jacket. I was trying to remember if I had taken the chicken out to defrost that morning. I was trying to remember if I had made a sandwich for Junior's lunch. I was trying to remember if I had eaten at all that day.

"Did I ever tell you I used to live in the West End? Lakeshore West." He was looking out the window, fondling the edges of the train seat.

"In the city?"

"The exact opposite of here. Before they started with all those tall buildings, I lived in a small apartment, and it had a window from which I could see the water, like this. This is the strange thing about any pond or stream or ocean—much like this, it is the exact same water, same frequency, same movement, no matter where you're standing in the world."

"Are you sure about that? I would imagine that the water would be different in Asia than it is here."

"Water's water. No matter how you put it."

What do you do with a man who's desperately holding on?

"You talk about your lived experiences like they happened in a dream," I said, finally.

His words never felt sincere to me. If my father were a flower, it would be a flower we would overlook because of its beauty. It would be a flower we'd lose interest in, for its lack of complexity, lack of texture—no pricks, no thorns.

"Of course, baby," he offered, now drawing hearts on the cloudy window. "Memories come to you the same way dreams do, and for the same reason."

"But then how do you know you're not confusing the two."

"If you can place it in your future, that's how you know it's just a dream."

"So you can't see yourself ever looking at the water again? As you are now. Let's say tomorrow. Or in six or seven months from now."

He looked at me, and his face bent into a wounded grin. "How's school going? Almost done freshman year. I remember when you were just a baby, you know."

Of course you do. That's the only memory you have of me.

"I still have an entire semester left. We're reading *L'Étranger*. You said you liked that book."

"There is no love of life without despair about life."

He was quoting Camus. I think it was a defence mechanism. One that I adopted later in life, but differently. I would reference a good text or a poem to lighten the mood. He did it to distract from the unknown.

"What's the matter, baby? You don't talk to me anymore. You used to be so bright."

"Why do you do that all the time? You can't talk about having had a past with me when we've only known each other for, like, five years. How you can say I used to be anything, when I came to you fully formed?"

"Well, you couldn't speak English," he said, and laughed. "You couldn't do this—" he inverted his fingers within his palms and shook them in the air, as though they were maracas.

There's a moment in conversations when the light goes on and hovers on one person. Centre stage. Fixated. Muted with too many words. I froze. Not entirely sure where the anger came from. Though I didn't feel rage. I was just tired. I was just annoyed. We had passed our stop at Guildwood about ten minutes ago. Now we were heading towards the city, and there was no turning back. We were committed. The scenery was small houses, factories, brown buildings. There was still water, but you had to look for it.

Then we got off at Exhibition Place. I don't suppose that was the plan.

He held my hand. In public, to perform the correct role of Father and Daughter, he often held my hand. I didn't mind. But I didn't like it, either. I was a straight shooter. I was growing up too quickly and preferred the real and honest. It would have meant much more to me if he had taken me out of school and said, "Loli, we need to get to know each other," as opposed to pretending that we already did. All I knew were stories. So many stories of where he had been. So many stories of why he had left. He had permanent wrinkles around his mouth. Unusual. Most people only have wrinkles around their mouth if they're smiling. Or, alternatively, only if they're perpetually frowning. He was doing neither. He just talked and talked and talked. "Did I ever tell you about my first winter?" I think that my father had enough words in him to rewrite *Don Quixote*. His favourite book. Because he believed in so many of his stories, I never knew which one belonged to either one of us.

We sat in a coffee shop. Lakeshore was big. And endless. The streets narrowed and remained void of pedestrians. Being there felt like starting over. My father drank his coffee in silence. So did I.

"We're celebrating, baby," he offered, as if I should have known. "I got a new job. I can quit all the other ones. It's office stuff. The details would bore you. But the money is good." He wanted to impress me so bad. "The money is good. The money is very good. Maman can focus on her studies. Finally become a real nurse. It will be like old times."

I had so much to say. So much to object to. So many questions. But I worried my words would hurt him. So I smiled. And I tilted my head. And I let him fill the room with memories of me. I suppose he was trying to tell me that this was the great sacrifice. Him leaving after I was born. Him hustling through country after country. Him loving me. Him loving Mother. And in every anecdote, there was so much excitement. Even the mundane and the uninteresting. I looked more like him than I did Mother. And I had taken from him his fascination with the world. His interest in people. Perhaps I had taken some of his pain too. Though I didn't know it yet, and I wouldn't come to know it until it was too late.

I let my father speak because he spoke well. It was easy to mistake his voice for the voice of a siren: calm, quiet, brushing against the shore.

IF NOT HAPPINESS

Jolie insisted that she loved him, that the house felt quiet when he was around, that he tasted very warm, that she was happy. I believed her. Sometimes, when I would sneak inside her bedroom, I noticed how peaceful she slept, as though she was aging against time, becoming kinder and more soft-boned as the summer slipped away.

"You are certain that you love him?" I said.

We used words like "certain" and "particular" to make us sound older. Our mouths had gotten used to swallowing bad air—we found it felt good to spit out words that did not fit.

"Very certain," she said, walking over to the swing and sitting to face me, dragging on a cigarette.

"Tell me, what's it really like?" I said.

"You know, some men want too much from the world. That's the problem. Too many people want too much of it, and then they take until there is nothing else. But with Henry, I don't know. He doesn't want anything."

"How can you be so sure he wants you, then?"

"That's the thing—he has me, so it doesn't matter."

Her answers were vague. They had been vague all summer.

I asked her again what it's like.

"It's like the first day after you wake up recovered from a cold."

I asked her if he touched her.

"To my core, Mermie, to my core."

Jolie started to call me Mermie because I once had a dream that she was a mermaid. We were ten or eleven at the time. She pulled down her drawers to show me that she was in fact not a mermaid. She grabbed my fingers and said, "Feel for yourself."

"I hate it when you call me Mermie."

"I get it. I hate it when Henry calls me Jolietta."

"It's not the same thing. That's your real name."

"Yeah, but Gigi was cracked out when she named me. Does that even count?"

I wasn't sure, so I sat silently and watched her finish the cigarette. It was getting colder, but neither one of us had anywhere else to go.

Henry came into Jolie's life by accident. She was home alone one day when he let himself in, asking for directions. Jolie was stretched out on her bed. She looked up and a man was watching her from the hallway. She said hi, and his face reddened.

"I must've got the wrong house."

"I could have sworn I locked the door. How did you get in?" Jolie said, tilting her head slightly to get a better look at him. He had greased hair and a premature mustache—a handsome man.

"The door was open. I am looking for a fellow, his name is Turner."

"Wait, your dad?" I said, exhaling smoke and grabbing Jolie by the hand.

We were walking to the park, where we spent most of our nights. It was close enough to where we lived that we could rush home in case of an emergency, far enough that nobody who looked could ever find us.

"Let me finish," Jolie said. "'I don't know anyone by that name,' I said, and he offered to take me out for coffee."

"That story is unbelievable."

"I know, but it truly happened that way. I pretended to like the coffee, but he was watching me closely and caught on. He said, 'How about I get you some milk and some sugar, Jolietta?' His tongue smacking his palate on that ending consonant."

"You sound like the girls in the movies."

"Who knows, maybe I am."

When we got to the park, we took cans of Pabst from our bags and sat on the swings. The seats were tiring; the heads of the bolts were rounded, causing the chain to get stuck. We never really sat to swing. Mostly just to pass time. Just to share a cigarette and watch people turning off their lights.

"How many of us do you think will end up in the same school this fall?" I said.

"Dylan got kicked out, did I tell you? Got caught for selling. It's just me now. And then you, I guess."

"Scary."

She squeezed my hand and said, "Henry said it's best not to associate myself with the kids from around here. That they might bring trouble."

"Does he know that you are the worst of the worst? I say this in awe of you, really."

"That's the thing. He knows. He knows everything."

I wanted her to go into detail. I wanted to know if his face lit up when he heard that Jolie had called the cops on her father, that Turner had been on the run ever since. I wanted to know if Henry was the one buying the cigarettes, and the brandy, and the fall sweaters, and the sneakers. I pictured the two of them holding hands in public, four towns over, kissing and laughing in boutiques, where the owners might question her age, and his, might stare at how white her skin was, how her curls swallowed her face and all you saw in the middle of all that chaos was a raised nose.

Jolie said, "This neighbourhood could use less trouble anyways. Don't you think Mrs Broomfield is happy I'm no longer *borrowing* her lipstick when she's away."

"You and Henry should start your own trespassers company. Call it Lovers Who Intrude, or Intruding Lovers."

"When did you get so smart, Mermie? Who taught you these big words?"

I wanted to tell her she taught me everything I knew. Instead, I pulled on my cigarette even longer.

We went back to our housing complex.

"Sometimes we don't even have sex. We just fall asleep with our faces glued together," she said. We were making mac and cheese from Mrs Broomfield's pantry. "He's super deep and serious."

"A romantic," I said.

"No," she said. "He's a realist."

I met Henry for the first time the night of my fifteenth birthday. He picked us up at the park, in a car that I later found out was expensive. It was white and had leather seats. I asked Jolie if it meant anything to her that our mothers couldn't drive, that they didn't even have licences, yet she had spent the last two months driving around in a Mustang.

"Jesus, I'm not that cynical," she said, pushing my braids behind my ears. "Of course it means something. It means that I'm not going to end up like them. And as soon as you get rid of these braids, maybe you won't either." She kissed me on the mouth. "Chin up," she said.

Henry had more hair than I expected. On his top lip, a pair of bushy brows, an entire grass field slapped across the bottom half of his face. When he got out of the car and waved, I gave Jolie a look that said, *You didn't tell me he was a hundred years old*. In turn, she gave me a look that said, *Stand up straight and stop acting your age*.

"You must be Mermie," he said.

"God, she told you that story."

"I understand the confusion. I thought she was a mermaid too."

"I'm sure you did," I said, deciding that no matter how well tonight went, I hated him.

"All right, people, less staring more walking," Jolie said.

"So, I hear you also live on Galloway," Henry said.

"As in, the government housing. That's correct. I see you drive a fancy car."

"A Mustang! A Mustang that is dying to take us anywhere!" Jolie said, hopping in the passenger seat, giving me a final look: *If you fuck this up for me, you're dead*.

"It's a nice car."

"Thanks. It's not a terrible neighbourhood, despite what you may think."

"Oh? You know what I may think?"

"Jolietta says you've been planning your big escape since the day you met."

"It's Jolie."

Henry and I were quiet the rest of the ride. Jolie told him about the complex. About the time her mother nearly burned their house down with a match and a bottle of gin, so we made a fort at the park and slept there until the smoke cleared. About how we got free cigarettes from the guy at the convenience store on Galloway and Lawrence because we caught him masturbating on shift. About the time Jolie asked a homeless man how it felt to be homeless and he said, "Much the same as having a house but without the home." Henry and I laughed even when the stories got sombre. It was impossible not to. Jolie had wit. She was facetious. It was comforting. She told Henry that, most importantly, the kids on the block took her in like one of their own.

"That's because poverty doesn't know race," I said.

Jolie turned around, undid her seat belt, leaned in until our noses were touching. "Even so," she said, "family is family," brushing my braids behind my ear, kissing me wet on the mouth. When she settled back in her seat, Henry smirked. He had hit the jackpot and we all knew it.

We went in through the alley of a pink building on Bathurst, then up two flights of stairs, then down a hall that led us inside a tiny room, with a sofa, a glass coffee table, red walls.

"Is this where you take all your victims?"

"Birthday girl's a little cranky because she needs a smoke," Jolie said.

"Only on special occasions."

"Hey, Henry. What do you call a male cougar?"

Henry slipped a cigarette in my mouth. "Don't worry," he said. "Jolietta is the only one for me."

I wanted to ask how old he was. Where exactly did he plan to take this relationship? But he pulled her in, pressed his palm on the small of her back, and suddenly, it made sense. Jolie smiled as though she was breathing for the first time. I got settled on the sofa and sucked on the cigarette. They danced, and then they laughed. Even today, remembering her at fourteen, she never looked more like herself.

"Henry, she's lonely, dance with her," Jolie said.

He took me in his arms and held me like he had been holding her. He said, "See, everything is just fine."

Before midnight, he pulled out a cake from the mini fridge and lit a candle. He told me to blow and watched closely as I did, as though he didn't believe that I would.

Back at the park, Jolie and I stretched out on the grass. Jolie scratched my scalp, ran her fingers through the spiderweb of my braids. She asked me what I thought of her boyfriend, and I took a moment to consider this.

"Isn't he a little old?" I said.

She smiled. "It's not that simple. Well, happy birthday, Mermie. Fifteen is a godawful year, but you've got me."

I suddenly realized that my life prior to this day was misleading. That Jolie would make it out of here because she didn't belong anywhere in particular.

I decided that when I got home, I'd take out my braids.

For dinner, Mother fried tilapia fish. She served this with rice, lemon, salt, and water. My brother, Junior, picked at his fish, stabbing it with a fork and eating only the parts that looked cooked.

Mother served herself a small portion, put the tail end of her fish in a container for my lunch tomorrow. Told us about work. The usual: an old man with white hair thought that she was his slave, called her "Annabette, the pretty Negro," and when he became lucid in the middle of his speech, he said, "How wonderful to see you bright and early this morning. How high is the sun today?" Mother laughed, squeezed him by the hand, and said, "Hello, Mr Roberto. If you please, I can take you for a walk down the ravine before the day shift is over." But by the time she got permission, she had become his slave again.

Junior reminded Mother that he'd "knock the man dry" if he were her.

"You don't go finding trouble with folks who don't know their ass from their mouth."

"Besides, Junior," I said, "you're five feet tall and still sleep with a night light."

"Don't let your food go cold, baby," Mother said.

"She's upset because her girlfriend got a boyfriend."

"Who? Jolietta? She the one bringing that white man around? How old is he?"

"You realize Jolie is basically, like, thirty-five, right?"

"A girl's a girl. Ain't no need to rush that."

My brother changed the topic. He was being considered for a scholarship. I could tell he expected me to get even more upset, but he saw right away that I hadn't been listening, so we ended our meal in silence.

Jolie did not come by the park that night, or the night after that. A month went by and I was deep in my sophomore year. When I asked her mother, Gigi, if she'd seen her, she looked up from the kitchen floor where she had found refuge.

She said, "Chi cerchi?"

With the little Italian I knew I told her I was looking for her daughter, Jolie. Jolietta? You know, super tall, super lean, super perfect?

Gigi looked at me and said, "When you find her, tell that bitch she owes me rent."

I had no idea Gigi was using again. Later, my mother said she'd been fired from the nursing home. Got caught stealing syringes. To which Jolie would say, "Jesus, Gigi, class, baby. You don't steal from the hand that feeds you," pushing what was left of Gigi's hair behind her ear.

The semester was coming to a close, and I had forgotten how to speak. When teachers would ask me questions, I would nod and smile. When girls would make comments about how coarse my hair was, I would nod, just nod. When my mother asked about Jolie, I would try to nod, but by then, nodding had become difficult.

On the last day before the holidays, I went by the park. The swings were covered with snow. The snow seemed higher than necessary, as though a kid was hiding underneath. I lit a cigarette. I forgot how to smoke. I tried to inhale, but I swallowed instead. I tried to spit out the tar, but I began to cry. An hour went by. Two hours.

I decided to swing when it got dark enough that I could pretend I was fucking the night. I was giving it all I had, really trusting my body. I could hear Jolie's voice clearly: "You trying to pop your cherry on a swing, Mermie?"

I kept going and going. And then I went home.

By February, I learned how to be extra fine. If you stand close enough to a window and it's raining, you can feel the drops pierce your skin. The illusion is spectacular. If you sleep with the lights on, you're never truly alone. Now I had lunch by the window in the open cafeteria. I calculated how long it would take the creek behind the school to melt, because on that particular day, I was most certainly fine.

I looked up and Jolie was walking towards me, her hair now pinned straight, her jeans dark and skinny, her shirt dry-cleaned.

I wouldn't have recognized her if I hadn't had her nose copyrighted.

"Oh, Mermaid, my Mermaid!"

"Jolie?"

"How I've missed you, my Mermie."

Jolie grabbed my face and kissed me. She slipped her tongue inside my mouth as if to say, "Good morning," with a background orchestra. I immediately forgot my plans to gouge her eyes when she came back. Then she skimmed my cheeks with her thumbs.

She said, "I've gotta go deal with the guidance counsellor and figure out my life. But, tonight, same place? Same time? Jesus, Merms, your breasts are in full! Where have they been all my life?"

Merms—whoever that was—was not fine.

Jolie up and disappeared, leaving me to look around the cafeteria for evidence that she had truly been there.

"Before you say anything, I'm not pregnant, or drugged up. I haven't stolen from a bank. I do not have any STIs—that I'm aware of—and I do not know how long I'm staying."

"Okay," I said.

"I'll tell you a secret, though. I showered. I mean, really, showered. I bathed. I spent hours and hours under water. I used real shampoo and shaved my hooch."

"Your hooch?"

"My bush."

"You haven't answered my question. What's it like? Really?"

"Jesus, you perv. I am talking about love, that's the good stuff. Nothing else matters. There is love and there is a willingness for happiness. The rest is child's play."

"Well, that was pretty cliché."

"I was being romantic."

I was happy I didn't have to explain myself. For a moment, we could pretend nothing had changed between us.

"You suck as a romantic."

"I did the best I could."

Your best was literal dog shit. I didn't say this, out of fear she might agree and I would have to live with knowing that she loved me, but only enough to serve me dog shit. I thought of what she would have said if I had been the one who left for what felt like a decade. Then I was immediately angry with myself for the perpetuating itch I felt to imitate her. The itch began in my head and spread to my mouth, then to my arm, then to my breast. It ended where her hands used to poke.

"You've got balls, and that's a good thing," she would say. "But don't ever try that shit again." Eating me up and spitting me right out.

The next day, Jolie lit both our cigarettes.

I asked, "How was it?" "Does the age gap worry you?" "Is there true consent?" And "Are you happy?"

She answered, "Fine." "Sometimes." "Sure." And "I don't know," which was strange to hear because she had always been very certain about everything.

We watched the houses on the other side of the intersection and behind the forest. Four rows of peeling townhomes glued together like one large building that survived a fire but couldn't afford a rebuild.

Jolie said that Gigi was gone when she got home last week, left the stovetop on low, vomit in every room.

"You can stay with me if you want."

"Thanks, but Henry has a place downtown. Besides, your mom certainly hates me."

"Mom doesn't hate anybody in particular. Except maybe Mr Roberto."

"She has a warm way of showing it."

"Yes, well, she came from nothing."

"We come from nothing," she said.

I wanted Jolie to hold me like she often did, to apologize, or to at least push my hair behind my ears. Our shoulders could have been brushing against each other, but the distance between us had become both literal and figurative. I couldn't bring myself to look at her. Instead, I looked at the houses beyond, hers and mine, awkwardly existing where everything else had been destroyed.

Spring came early and unexpectedly. Jolie took a job as a nanny downtown. She babysat for a friend of a friend of a friend of Henry's. He did not seem to mind that her breasts were slightly deflated. And her throat and her arms and her legs were smaller than ever before. She even spoke less.

But, one afternoon, the sun came out full force. Jolie suggested we go to the beach. "It's really tender this time of the year."

"All right," I said, happy to have her want to do something—anything.

Henry, of course, had become a character in our lives, almost fatherly in some ways. He answered whenever she called; he bought groceries and drove us around. He even fixed things around the house for my mother. We watched from my porch as a new family moved in where Jolie and Gigi had lived. We stood silently, wondering where Gigi had gone but knowing that, like Jolie, she might ultimately come back. We all agreed without agreeing that everything was fine.

At the beach, Henry spread a large picnic blanket underneath an equally large umbrella. The water was very blue, unlike what I expected. It seemed to begin where the sky ended, or was it the other way around? Jolie stood on the shore looking more like an image than an actual person. She belonged beyond the water. It crept at her feet, then tumbled away gently when she lifted her toes. Her hair blew in the wind like a sailboat. The entire world was waiting to see if she would run inside the tide and never come out.

Henry lay next to me on the blanket, reading. It occurred to me then that he often read, sometimes out loud when we would go for coffee, sometimes quoting lines from poems we later googled. The book rested on his gut so that I couldn't see the cover. He was shirtless but wore white pants. His premature facial hair was now a bush slapped across his face. Every so often he looked up, as if to make sure Jolie hadn't been blown away or something.

"What are you reading?"

"*Invisible Man*," he said. "Have you heard of it?"

I hadn't. But I began to enjoy the lexicon he used to talk about the things he loved. "No," I said, "What's it about?"

"A man who is rendered invisible by the colour of his skin."

"I can relate," I said, shifting my look from him to Jolie.

"Really? I see you just fine."

"It's not that. I just mean, well, look at her."

So we both looked at Jolie in silence.

"Not even the ocean can compare."

"Now you must've taken that line from a bad poetry book," he said, straightening himself to be an inch away from my face. "Does she know?"

"It's Jolie," I said. "She knows everything."

I looked around and realized that this was my first time on a beach. My first sand experience. My first ocean. It was cool and balmy, white. Everyone on the beach looked happy.

Henry got up and ran towards Jolie, scooped her up and threw her over his shoulders. She giggled, made a soft moan, exactly like in the movies. Only now we were living it. Sand and all.

I spent the night at Henry's apartment, where Jolie lived. Henry was a photographer—I was finding this out now. His loft apartment was all windows. I kind of thought he was a rich guy with a little-girl fetish. But now, the man behind the Mustang was just a man who was in love with a girl, or something.

Jolie and Henry stretched out on the bed. But then Jolie began to unzip his pants while I stood there. She reached down and ran her tongue along the side of his face. I didn't know what to do, so I crawled in bed with them. Jolie took me in her arms, and I had almost forgotten what that felt like. And then it was Henry touching me. I had an idea of what this was, but I wasn't entirely sure, so I shut my eyes and remembered Jolie and me underneath the covers all those years, our bodies morphing into one, then her fingers finding their way inside of my everything.

When I opened my eyes again, it was just me and Henry naked on the mattress. He was sleeping, or pretending to. I did not know how long Henry and I had been alone like this. I heard my heart beating against the concrete walls like gunshots. I took a blanket, a duvet, or a comforter, something, and ran out on the balcony.

I whispered her name, and there she was, naked.

"Are you cold?" I asked.

"Hi, Mermie."

I listened to the sound of the city settling in for the night. "What's going on?"

"What do you mean?"

"You're distant."

"Isn't distance a state of mind?"

"You're answering my questions with questions."

"That's definitive."

"Something's wrong."

She stared at the buildings with their lights perpetually on as if they had something that belonged to her. "I can't live like this anymore."

"Jolietta, please!" I said this, and then it occurred to me that I had been weeping in distress. Messy and childlike. I'm not entirely sure when the crying began, but now it was uncontrollable. Jolie pressed on her face, checking for tears that were supposed to be there but wouldn't come.

"Tell me something, please, anything," I said. Somewhere between the sobbing and the holding my breath and the shutting my eyes and the throwing of myself on the floor, I remembered that Jolie wanted happiness, and this was not it.

I woke up the next morning in Henry's bed. I was dressed. I did not remember dressing, but I lay there in a silk slip, my nipples glued to the fabric. Henry sat on the bottom of the bed finishing *Invisible Man*. He made coffee and played something he later confirmed was Led Zeppelin.

"Turn it off," I said and he did.

I could tell how bright the sun was because of how spacious the apartment felt. Henry gave me a bowl of fruit and added milk to my coffee. He watched me very closely, as though afraid I would stop breathing if he looked away.

"Stop staring," I said, not knowing myself to be so frank.

"Would you like me to drive you home?"

"No," I said.

I walked around the apartment and touched the walls, then I pounded my head against the wall. Henry held me for what felt like the entire day.

THIS IS ONLY TEMPORARY

After Darnell was beaten to death at the intersection of Galloway and Lawrence, everybody kept their doors unlocked, wide open.

Mrs Broomfield was putting extensions in my hair while we watched the news. She was a big black woman with snake hands. On the television, we heard that the complex where we lived was the ghetto of the poor. We heard that Darnell was a thug who had stolen some money from another thug, and his death was an accident of frustration. We heard that there were no witnesses, and that the criminals were still on the run. We heard that it might have been self-defence, because they found a small knife meant to clean underneath toenails hiding inside Darnell's pocket. We heard that Darnell was a high-school dropout who sold dope and fucked sex workers. We heard that Darnell came from a family of mentally ill people. On a different channel, we heard that government housing should be banned. We heard that Regent Park's revitalization plan was the best thing that could have happened to Toronto. And that Scarborough needed the same chance. We heard that immigrants were taking advantage of taxpayers' money. We heard that everybody should be on the lookout for two young black men in black hoodies. We heard that the residents of that area—our area—should stay indoors.

"Go see how good you look," Mrs Broomfield suggested.

I liked what I saw. The extensions were hand-picked by Mother. They curled at the bottom. A honey-blonde ombre. When I came back to the dining room, Mrs Broomfield was sweeping up fall-outs of my hair. I went over to help. "I got this, mama, thank you."

Just once in my life I called Mrs Broomfield something other than mama and she beat me with a broom and left me on the front yard.

I always ate with Mrs Broomfield when she was finished working on me. I was always her last client. I lived right next door. Most of the time I came by just to say hi, though. I'd go through her pantry and grab mac and cheese or Mr. Noodles if it was obvious that my parents wouldn't be home for a few days. Other times, I just sat in the living room while she knitted and watched TV. Most of the kids came around came for the TV. She was one of the only tenants who owed such a thing. She even had a radio in the kitchen window over the sink, and on summer days, she'd play it at full volume.

Mrs Broomfield didn't charge me for doing my hair, either. Mainly because I helped with groceries and cleaned when she was getting her nails done with her girlfriends. But I think it was an incentive to get me to come back. In Galloway, Mrs Broomfield was legend for witnessing the Rwandan genocide. Her attitude so much positivity and optimism, like, "This is a war, child, it's not going to last." I liked to apply that to everything else: this world is a war, this neighbourhood is a war, this street, this house, this body, this person, this feeling, this war.

Once, when Mother and I were fighting on the street, Mrs Broomfield came out and yelled at us both. Told Mother she should be ashamed of herself, and I think, for a week, she was. To me, Mrs Broomfield said, "Cut your shit. Hating on her ain't gonna change the fact that she is your mother. Go on, little girl, go on and apologize to the woman."

After I was done sweeping up my hair, I moved into the kitchen and helped Mrs Broomfield carry the sausage stew and potatoes to the dining room. She allowed me to have half a glass of wine per serving, not more. I paid attention to the way she ate her stew with her hands. Sometimes you might find her in one of the parking lots, smoking weed with the dealers. She was known for giving them a bed and soup, in exchange for work around the house. Mrs Broomfield was sixty-two years old. Never married. Never with child.

Never without company. When Dylan had gotten accepted to university on full scholarship, Mrs Broomfield grilled pig on a stick as a congratulations gift. The whole complex came together.

Jennifer let herself in. I knew her only a little bit. She was the neighbourhood tutor. She specialized in translation and was fluent in five languages.

"Hi, Jenny."

"Hi, mama."

"You hungry?"

The three of us ate. The conversation was light but full. Jennifer was due to graduate university. She didn't know what she wanted to be exactly or in what field, but she talked at length about enjoying school. The conversation didn't turn to Darnell until we were in the kitchen washing the dishes. And Omar had let himself in to bring Mrs Broomfield some pot brownies.

"Wasn't he studying on campus with you?" Omar asked Jennifer.

"Yeah, law and politics."

"That boy didn't deserve that," Mrs Broomfield said.

"Tyson saw the whole thing, you know, ma. They were after his headphones. Tyson hasn't gotten out of bed since."

"Do you think he'll talk?" Jennifer said.

"And put a target on his back? He has a kid, you know."

"You tell Ty if he needs somebody to talk to he comes to me."

Omar walked me home that night. "How's school going? Heard you're a sophomore now. At that private school."

"It's not private, it's just French."

"Right, right, Miss Frenchie. All I know is, voulez-vous coucher avec moi."

Mother was sitting on the steps when we arrived.

"Good evening, auntie," Omar said.

Mother just looked at him. And then looked at me. And then got up and disappeared into our house.

The next day, we had a neighbourhood barbecue. It had been planned long before Darnell's first rib was broken. It was our way of welcoming the summer. People brought garbage bags filled with clothes, and people looked for their children's sizes. I grilled tilapia on Mrs Broomfield's porch. It was stuffed with dill and paprika. But the winning meal was Nicki's butter chicken. She was telling us about Aunt Loretta, who hadn't stopped watering her plants since Darnell walked out the door that morning. "It's like nothing's changed," Nicki said.

We set up camp outside of Aunt Loretta's house. Nobody slept. Everybody traded stories. Everybody laughed. And once the parents went back inside, we got out of our sleeping bags and drank in honour of Darnell. The lights in Aunt Loretta's house remained on all night. We could see her reading on the sofa. Watching over us.

Darnell was in love with a boy named Cory. Some say this led to his death. Some say this is what kept him going when times got rough. Darnell used to go Christmas carolling by himself every July. We never knew when he'd come. We just knew that he would.

This was everybody's favourite story. He spent hours icing his ass afterwards: Darnell was the first kid Mrs Broomfield gave a whooping to.

I looked out into our street. It hadn't lost its colour. It hadn't lost its spirit.

In the weeks that followed, Mrs Broomfield was busier than ever. More moms left their toddlers with her now that Darnell was gone. The woman who cut people's grass had lowered her prices, and Jennifer organized a field trip to the bluff.

We crossed a few parks to get to the water. We sat on the beach, some adults, mostly kids. We played games all afternoon, and it was intense. Monopoly and Go Fish. When it got dark we made a fire. There were twenty to thirty of us toasting marshmallows for s'mores. Our parents didn't care how late we stayed because they knew we'd be safe. We were safest when we were together. Plus, Mrs Broomfield was there with us.

"What is the difference between this and a genocide?" she asked.

Nobody knew, but everybody understood.

PHYLLIS GREEN

I had a friend at school named Tiffani. I used to follow her around because she was beautiful and rich, and because she told me to. Tiffani sat in the front of the classroom. She wasn't smart. She wasn't good at much, but she won all the arts and crafts awards every year. Her parents would make generous donations to the school—this became obvious the year she won athlete of the year.

Tiffani and I first became friends when I was chubbier. But then I got skinny, and she told everybody that I was using cocaine and water to lose weight. I think she thought this would ruin my good-girl reputation, but it only made me more popular. I began to wear my hair really straight and roll my Catholic school kilt so that my ass cheek would show whenever I bent down. Obviously, I bent down quite often. It wasn't a matter of getting attention. The girls who kept to themselves were the ones constantly being scrutinized. This way, with my blouse unbuttoned and my high heels, I was just like everybody else.

By the time we were seniors, I was so thin Tiffani began to follow me. Nobody questioned my weight loss, and neither did I. I had just lost interest in sleep, hydration, and food. And things at home had gotten worse. My best friend Jolie had gotten her first real boyfriend and nobody knew where she went when she went away. Meanwhile, my father would lock himself in the bathroom and cry.

Tiffani was the only person who really knew me.

Tiffani was the only person who knew I lived on Galloway.

I knew her secrets too: every night, when her parents went to bed and the nanny left, Tiffani would sneak out. Every night, she went and got lost. She never walked the same street twice. The goal was to find new places to explore. The goal was to find someone who'd come for her. Sometimes, she'd sleep on a park bench. Other times, she'd hide behind a gas station. She wanted to be fucked. She'd never been touched before, and this was what she wanted.

We were sitting in her bedroom. It was the largest bedroom I'd ever seen in my life. It had pink decorations on the walls that made me uncomfortable.

"Drink?" she said, and gave me some Smirnoff Ice in a red cup. "I just want to know what it would be like."

"What what would be like?"

"To feel something."

I drank the Smirnoff.

"Hit me," Tiffani said.

"Are you crazy?"

"Yes, fucking hit me."

I poured more Smirnoff into both our cups.

"You're so lucky," she told me. "You've been through things."

One Monday in October, we got a transfer student from another French Catholic high school. Her name was Phyllis Green. She was sitting with us in the cafeteria, black and purebred but born in Canada. With us was Pamela.

"It was at Jane and Finch. West of Toronto. And north," Phyllis Green said.

"So you're a brainer?" Tiffani asked. She sipped all the juice from her straw. The very last drop made a swirl, and she turned it into something sexual.

All the other girls at the table were white, except for me and Phyllis Green. But before Phyllis Green, it had been just me. Tiffani and Pamela had told me that we would be "taking her under our wings"—but only if she could prove herself.

"Honestly," I said when the anticipation of Tiffani's question began to fade, "we've all done it."

It was a lie. I had only seen a cock once in real life. It was my brother's. And it was the worst experience of my entire life.

Phyllis Green reassured us that she was "not like that." And we laughed. I laughed even louder, knowing what was coming next.

"Well, we're going to have to fix that," Pamela said.

"I'm saving myself for marriage," Phyllis Green said.

"For God?" Tiffani asked, straw stuck between her front teeth.

"No," Phyllis Green persisted. "For marriage."

Most of us got to school early for the free breakfast. I got to school early for anything that was free. But today, Tiffani, Pamela, and I had gotten to school early as part of the welcoming committee. Mr Parfait had pushed me to participate. Said that I would be the ideal candidate to make Phyllis Green feel most at home. It couldn't be easy transferring in mid-October, he told me. But once Phyllis Green came out of the Toyota, wearing her skirt down to her knees and a second-hand cardigan, I understood what he really meant.

Before the bell rang, Phyllis Green leaned forward. "I didn't want to ask in front of them. They're so intimidating. What does brainer mean?"

I didn't like the way she had chosen me to be the one she leaned on. I didn't like the way she had created a barrier between us and them. And I especially didn't like the fact that I had never in my life considered Tiffani and Pamela to be "them." And myself to be "the other." I knew in that moment that Phyllis Green was doomed. There was nothing I could do to save her. And, frankly, I didn't want to. I enjoyed my ability to blend in. I was passing.

In the washroom, Pamela asked, "What kind of name is Phyllis Green anyways?" She brought the tip of the key to her nose and inhaled the cocaine.

"I think it's Muslim," Tiffani answered.

"Muslims can't be black?" Pamela asked.

Both girls looked at me. I looked at my reflection. Just like Tiffani, and just like Pamela. I wore light pink lipstick. Dark eyeliner in celebration of our collective grunge phase. "Don't look at me," I said.

"We should call her P.J.," Tiffani suggested.

"But Green is spelled with a *G*," I said.

"So?" they chorused.

"She kind of looks like a horse, don't you think?" Tiffani said.

"I mean, that mouth, right?"

A toilet flushed. Then the bell rang. We had biology next.

Outside, P.J. was waiting where I had told her to wait.

"So, where are you from?" she asked.

"What do you mean?"

"Like where are you from from?"

"Like where does my black come from?"

She giggled. "I guess."

I willed my stomach to tighten and took a deep breath and sat down. She sat next to me.

Mason passed a note from the back of the class, and it was addressed to me.

Does she suck dick?
Yes or No

I circled *Yes*, reached my arm to the person sitting next to me. Whoever it was, it wouldn't matter. We had a system. You passed the note to the person behind you or next to you or in front of you. You read it if you wanted, but the letter must always, always reach the person it was intended for.

Then, Mr Parfait: "How many times are we going to go through this?" He snatched it out of my twisted hand.

"I wouldn't read that if I were you," Mason said from the back of the class. He was beautiful like a mistake, with blond curls that could make you question his sexuality.

"Another love note, Mr Corner?"

Mr Parfait was living out his high-school fantasies. In this class, he was the king. In this class, he was God. This could have been true for most of the teachers. Desperate for affection. Getting off on the attention of fifteen-year-olds. Whenever I saw Mr Parfait for tutoring, it was only because I pitied him. It was only because he gave me falsified good grades. It was only because I was the only black girl in class. And he the only black teacher. And he played football with my father on Sundays. But something in the way he looked at me, and then at Phyllis, and then back at me, told me that I was about to lose my privileges.

"Really, Mr Parfait, you shouldn't read that. You'll get in trouble for it."

"Shut up, Mason," another boy from the back shouted.

I looked down at my hands. My hands. I could feel P.J. looking at me. I could feel her eyes glistening with excitement. Feeling like she was part of some holy tribe.

"Is that a threat, Mr Corner?"

"I'm just saying. What good do you get being involved in student affairs? There should be some boundaries. We should have the right to our privacy. Our right to communicate."

"All classroom communications should be collective. A question you have may be beneficial for somebody else. When I see these notes flying around class, I assume you're confused and too embarrassed to ask out loud. Am I right, Mr Corner?"

"You're putting me on the spot, Mr Parfait. This is intimidation."

Everybody laughed.

"Shall we answer your question together?"

And then Tiffani said, "I have a question, Mr Parfait."

"Yes, Tiffani?"

"Why are you such a fucking dick?"

"Yeah, I'd like to know too," Mason said.

And then a rehearsed chiming of yeahs and yeses broke out. P.J. was laughing too. I couldn't bear to look at her. But I could feel her energy. I could feel every part of her.

We were saved by the bell. Everybody ran out of the classroom, pushing and shoving to get through the door. I was glued to my seat. P.J. stood hovering in front of me with her fucking big eyes.

"Just leave. Just go away." I had peed myself just a little. But I didn't know how little was a little. So I sat. And I waited. And then it was just me and Mr Parfait. He had read the note.

"What should I do about this, Loli?"

"I don't feel well." My hands. My wrinkled, dry, hot hands.

"This is grounds for a suspension."

"I didn't write it."

"But you participated."

"I wasn't the only one."

"Loli, I can't protect you if you won't let me."

Mr Parfait walked towards me. I leaned forward so that his breath was all I could inhale. *Do I tell him I peed myself? Or do I wait until he's gotten too close and scream?* Finally, I looked up. He had a soulful smile. The only thing worse than making a man angry was disappointing him.

"I can't help you if you won't let me," he said again, and I snapped.

"You're not my fucking father."

So Mr Parfait went and got me a new school skirt and gym shorts to wear as underwear. I don't know why he was always so kind to me. I couldn't tell if it was genuine or sexual. I tried not to make everything about sex, every act of kindness, every well-wish, every hello. But you go through life being touched, you go through life being looked at, you go through life with an uncle commenting on your breasts, or your brother's friend giving you a condom for your birthday then denying it, you go through life being called a cunt on public transportation, you go through life being followed at midnight, you go through life being told you're pretty, you're pretty, you're so fucking pretty—it gets complicated.

In the cafeteria, I was hit with déjà vu. I remembered my first year here, my first time sitting right there, in that exact spot. On a day much like today. Except now, instead of me, it was P.J., shy but overcompensating with loud laughter. Tiffani forcing interest, tilting her head to the left and then to the right like clock arms. And Pamela, high.

When Tiffani saw me, she got up and ran towards me. "Okay, we're doing it."

"Doing what?"

"You know—with P.J."

"What are you talking about?"

"Mason, obviously. You know he has low-key jungle fever, right? I mean, you should know, wink, wink, nudge, nudge."

I didn't. Mason had never looked at me. And for that I was grateful.

Tiffani whistled and Pamela looked up and said something that must have excited P.J. because she got up too, all smiles.

Years ago, before any of us were born, a student had killed himself behind the staircase in the west end of the building. Nobody knew why. The school closed down and reopened a few months later, introduced a French division to help everyone forget. Now, the staircase remained mostly vacant, as if suicide were somehow contagious.

It was Tiffani, Pamela, and me, and Mason and P.J.

"What? Are we gonna smoke pot?" she asked.

"We aren't going to do anything, silly," Pamela said.

"Think of it like an initiation," Tiffani said.

"Hi, Phyllis," Mason said. "You know you're really pretty, Phyllis. Isn't she pretty, guys?"

"Loli, can you keep a lookout?" Tiffani said.

I went and stood by the doors. I could see parts of them but not clearly. The staircase took up most of my vision. And the bright light from the floor-to-ceiling windows, which stretched all the way to the third floor, was emasculating. They were whispering now, and I was thinking of nothing. Or the opposite of nothing. Which is everything. But when you're thinking of everything altogether, it's like having no thoughts at all. From here, the school looked peaceful. The emptied halls, newly waxed, looked clean and never used before.

All I could see of Tiffani and Pamela were their backs. Mason was pinned against the window, the light making a halo around his head, glowing wings around his body. He was moaning. The halls were safe. We were safe. I walked around the staircase, following a stench. Like spoiled perfume or expired eggs. A wet odour.

"That's a good girl," I heard someone say.

Tiffani and Pamela were holding P.J.'s hair. Her long braids like a tied rope. They used their knees to keep her arms wrapped behind her back. And Mason motioned her head forward and backwards—towards him, towards me, towards him, towards me, towards him.

My body weakened, and I leaned against the wall. And then I was on the ground too, holding myself up the best way I could. I watched until it was over. Then, he cleaned himself. Mason zipped his pants and smiled. He patted Tiffani on the back, kissed Pamela on the forehead.

"'Sup, Lo," he said, as he walked past me, disappearing behind the fogged-up glass doors.

I don't remember what happened afterwards. I blacked out. I fell asleep. I went elsewhere. I was so tired. I remained, my fingernails attempting to travel through the brick wall. I'm not sure when they left. I just know that the bell rang for third period. And then it rang for fourth period.

I found Tiffani in the parking lot. I didn't know where to start. I didn't even know what I wanted to start. But I felt sick. And I thought that she was sick. And—

"Need a ride, babe?" Tiffani asked. "Momski should be here in, like, two secs."

"What was that?" I heard myself ask.

"What was what?"

"You made her—"

"Dude, you said it yourself, everybody does it. Also, I didn't *make* anyone do anything."

"You were holding her hair."

"It's wild fucking hair."

"I never did that."

"Of course not, babe, you're one of us, 'kay?"

I didn't know what that meant. I didn't know what anything meant. Tiffani's mom arrived and they left. I waited in the parking lot until late. I watched every teacher get inside their car. I declined every offer for a ride home. I felt dizzy and fever-ridden. Whatever I was feeling, I couldn't imagine what it must have been like for P.J. I mean, for Phyllis. For Phyllis Green.

"Hi, Loli," she said to me the next day. "Trust you had a nice night?"

"What was last night?" I answered.

"I'm just making small talk."

Phyllis Green looked happy. Phyllis Green looked normal. Phyllis Green had the biggest eyes I had ever seen—the roundest nose. Her jaw was sharp, and her hairline was receding. Phyllis Green had cheekbones that looked like implants. She had untamed eyebrows. Phyllis Green had the body of an athlete. And arms she kept close to her body.

I watched her walk away. She disappeared into a classroom and I just stood there.

TEN-YEAR REUNION

I knew my father was dead the moment I walked into the bedroom. Still, I walked towards his side of the bed. I looked for the sleeping pills, which he kept on the nightstand, behind the Bible. I knew the pills wouldn't be there. But still, I looked. I looked because I was high. I was so high that I had to decide whether to call the ambulance now, or after a shower, or in the morning, after I'd gotten some rest. But then I remembered that I'd never fallen asleep on cocaine, so I took a bath instead. I called the ambulance from the tub.

I called my brother next.

"I have to tell you something."

"It's four a.m., Lo."

"I know. I'm so surprised you answered."

I told Junior that I had done seven Hollywoods and that I was sorry for it. My brother was caring. Always willing to search that beautiful brain of his for some optimism. In my high, I kept trying to touch my nose with my tongue, while still going on and on and on about how I really didn't mean to get this fucked up, but it just helps with the noise. *So much noise, Junior.* I had been candid once before with my brother. And then I ignored him for several months. And now I was looking ahead at my future, and I knew it would be a year before I spoke to my brother again, after tonight, after this phone call.

Then I heard a banging on the door. And then I heard a scream down the hall. It was Mother. I told Junior I had to go and hung up.

Mother didn't cry at the sight of her dead husband. I had never seen Mother cry, and I felt a bit relieved not to have to suffer through it now for the first time. Not like this. I listened to her hurling. And then she began to sing. All gospel. Songs I recognized from other people's deaths. Then I could hear footsteps. A marching band. A herd of bulls. Sirens. Men entering the house. I could hear somebody attempting to reason with Mother, and I could hear her insisting on a moment of praying, please. Somebody said a lot of things to Mother, or to the men, or to me. And then I heard, "Shut up, shut the fuck up, shut it, please." And for a moment, the house did get quiet.

Mother found me in the tub three hours later. She opened the bathroom door slowly, as though she knew I had been there all along. I was terrified. She'd see that my nipples were pierced. She'd see that I had been shaving my bush. She'd immediately associate the pierced nipples and the shaved pussy with sex. We'd get into a heated argument. It would end with me leaving the house, slamming the door behind me. It would end with her throwing my clothes in the yard. I could see it all so clearly.

"Your father's dead," she announced.

"How?" I asked.

I wanted to hear her say it.

"In his sleep."

Mother closed the door on her way out. The water was cold. But not freezing I heard her walk to her bedroom. Though she mustn't have closed the door behind her, because the door makes this sound. Like a mouse. Like a rooster in the morning. It was then that I realized I hadn't put any soap in my bath. Hadn't put any bubbles. So I reached for the shampoo, and then I felt satisfied. Fatigue would hit me any moment. In two or three more hours, fatigue would come. The waiting was painful, like waiting for air to fill cupped hands.

I found Mother frying bacon. She wore her hair pushed back in a high bun. I hadn't seen so much of her face in such a long time. She looked quite like herself.

"Going back to the morgue later," she said.

"Why? Haven't they already ruled the cause of death? Didn't you already identify the body?"

"Your father?"

"Yeah, sorry. That's what I meant."

She knew I was coming down. She knew I had been in the bag, but so long as she didn't address it, we could pretend.

"Do you want me to come with you?"

"You have school."

"True."

She finished with the bacon and ate it from the pan. Strip after strip. And she ate it naked, without any bread or toppings. Then, she kissed me. She left for the day. And I left for school. I didn't want to go, but I figured I'd be able to score some pills. Perhaps I could then come home for some sleep.

I walked by Mrs Broomfield. She was sitting on her lawn, throwing salt on the sidewalk. The snow baked quickly overnight, causing the pavement to glisten. She didn't give me sad eyes. She just kept making her lawn chair rock like a baby's cradle.

I suppose she'd seen the whole thing. I suppose she'd watched my father get carried out to the ambulance, the paramedics moving too slowly so as to not step on a crack, or a branch, or some ice and, you know, drop the dead. And I suppose she knew too, without needing the confirmation, that it was my father. And that there was no way he could have been saved. And that it was only a matter of time before he was successful.

I found Mason behind the staircase in the west side of the school. He sold me some Xanax and Klonopin, and then he asked if I'd give him something in return. Normally, I'd say no, but I was suddenly a person in reduced circumstances.

"Not bad," he told me. He always told me that I was not bad, never that I was good. Mason reminded me to mix the Xanax with a bit of melatonin but to take the pins straight. This too was part of my circumstances—I had two options. One that would shock my body and one that would lay me down. Both leaving me worse off than I already was.

I went home without speaking to anyone. Nobody was on our street. And, of course, nobody was home. I only took a third of a Xanax. It was stronger than the stuff my father took, and I didn't want to be asleep that long. I was terrified that if I slept too long, I'd miss it. I'd miss all of it.

Almost every dream I had was a memory of my father and me. And in every single one we were playing this game where I was a princess. In one of the dreams, we were at a tea party. It was my birthday. I was six or seven. He let me dress him up as a princess too, and I told him he looked just as beautiful as a little girl. He told me something extra lame, like, "Je pourrais mourir pour toi." I woke up instantly. It was six p.m. I could hear that the house was empty but figured Mother was in the basement doing laundry.

I found her in the kitchen. She looked like she hadn't moved since this morning. Under each eye, she had moisturizer. Hydrating gel. She still cared about her beauty. And her youth. She was eternal.

"You're awake," she said.

"Surprise, surprise."

"Okay, you should freshen up."

"When will Junior get here?"

"Haven't called him yet. Maybe when I have an idea of the funeral stuff."

"Do you have enough money for that? I mean, I have some saved up."

"We'll figure it out."

And that was that. That was the most Mother and I would ever talk about it.

I was still feeling buzzed and dragged out. Mother and I sat on the front steps. The night was good. And the sky so clear, empty of all its wonders, divorced from the stars, autonomic of the moon. The sky was usually so full this far east of the city, and I seldom missed the opportunity to watch it dissolve.

I pulled out a cigarette and lit up in front of Mother. It was one of the scariest things I had ever done. But given my circumstances, I trusted I would get away with this too. Mother made her fingers into a peace sign. This was smoker's lingo for *Give me one.* I gave Mother the one I had been working on. Lit a new one for myself. When she exhaled, I wondered if it was the first time she had done that.

"He wanted to paint the porch red." Mother coughed a little in between each draw. "You know, like the gates in Kinshasa."

"That would have made no sense. It wouldn't have gone with anything."

"Yeah, but you know your father."

"He's so fucking weird, right?"

"He's just nostalgic."

"The last thing he said to me, when I was leaving last night, was that he'd see me in ten years. He was like, 'On se donne rendez-vous dans dix ans?' And I was like, sure whatever."

Mother laughed. "That's a song. I mean, it's his favourite song."

"What?"

"You know the one. By Patrick Bruel."

Mother sang parts of the song.

Now I was laughing too. "He's so lame. He's such a weirdo."

Before bed, I crushed some Xanax for Mom. Tonight, she was Mom. She was soft.

We removed the sheets from her bed. We slept on the naked mattress. Of course, the smell was pronounced. But, fuck it: we let our bodies sink deep through the covers, deep through the second floor, deep through the basement, deep until we were in the ground. Underneath all that dirt.

The next morning, he was still dead, but not like an exclamation point, like a set of ellipses. I was still coming down from my weeklong binge. I could never be satisfied with just one line. Or just one drink. Or just one kiss. I was the most like my father.

Last minute, I decided not to apply for university.

It was mid-December. I thought a funeral during the holidays would be depressing. And all the light in the world—we could use some of that. I told Mother, "What if we had the funeral in the new year. What if we waited for spring?"

"That feels like a drag."

"But do you really want to make people come out just before Christmas?"

"It won't be a funeral. You know your aunts—it'll be a celebration."

"What if we just cremated the body and waited until Junior finishes his semester?"

"You want to wait four months to have a funeral?"

"Sure, why not? Junior won't be able to handle all of this. He'll be hysterical. He won't make it through."

"So we burn his body, and then what?"

When Mother and I spoke, we'd change positions. I would become the one with all the answers. She would remain the one with all the questions. But this time I had no answer. And this time she had no questions. We both just knew what we knew.

My father's body was cremated the next day. I came home from school and he was sitting in a gold urn on top of the coffee table.

In my room I had a bit of cocaine left, but I didn't want to do any of it. Still, it took a lot of convincing to get me not to do it. I flushed it down the toilet. And then I noticed the water in the tub from seventy-two hours ago was rotten now. I left it there. Death is slow. It takes a long time to settle. It feeds from the inside, like a fetus. Death is like being pregnant and never giving birth.

I took a taxi to a bar. Everybody looked decent. Not happy but not not happy. They talked to each other, mindless and distracted. Old men, mostly in their late fifties and sixties, sat on the wood and discussed their wives, and their cottages. Like they were interchangeable. That's when I saw Dylan.

Ocean-eyed Dylan.

He recognized me too. Walked up to me with a grin. Last I saw Dylan, he was a little boy. Now I was standing in front of a fully realized man. The kind women in Galloway would pray their sons would turn out to be. Where had time gone? Why hadn't it told us it would be leaving? Had I been in love with Dylan too? Maybe once.

"You're so—"

"Skinny?" I interrupted. I had gotten tired of hearing it.

"But more than that."

"Thanks, you look well too. You've always looked well, but now you look very well."

The conversation flew between us. No tension. No bumps. No stopping to wonder if rekindling old euphoria could stop new growth. Dylan didn't live in my neighbourhood, but he used to hang around there all the time. When he was much younger. Before the facial hair.

After last call, I took Dylan to a cemetery. It was next to the water. You could smell it. Icy, with a burn. Good in the air. Good everywhere. We walked around for hours and he not once asked what or why or how come. Then I saw a headstone that I liked. It looked like it could belong to my father. It was grey and simple. It just had a name and a date. No fuss. No show. No party. Just the truth. I loved that gravestone so fucking much. I stood there, loving it for some time.

Then I was pulling Dylan towards me and walking backwards towards the gravestone.

"Did you ever met my father, Dyl?"

"He was always in and out, but I saw him around. Such a happy man."

"You think he was happy?"

"He seemed like it."

Then, Dylan and I fell silent.

I slipped my hands inside of his. They were cold but stern. He held me tightly.

"You know he killed himself, right?" I asked Dylan.

"I know," he said.

I didn't look to see his reaction, but I could imagine it was accepting. I didn't bother to ask how he knew. News travels fast. Even news that isn't news and is just a matter of fact. I could picture everybody from church praying all at once. I could hear it echo into the night—God called on him, and he solemnly obeyed. That was the story, and though it was a falsified story, it was the one that would get us through the next ten years.

I pulled Dylan close to me, and I kissed him. I stretched out on the cold grass and opened my legs for him. Without hesitation, he pulled down my underwear and mounted me. He stroked deeply enough to sober me up completely. Still, I moaned "Daddy," as if I was supposed to feel exceptionally close to him now but couldn't.

Afterwards, we sat where I had bled and where he had come. We listened to the noises that the night made: hearts beating, cars racing, people in the distance.

THERESA IS GETTING MARRIED

My cousin Theresa got married a month after my father was cremated. She got married to a guy she met the night before her wedding day. She was nineteen years old and pregnant. She was not allowed to have the baby—and be uneducated and unmarried. My cousin Theresa had to agree to marry, and to get an education, and then, only then, the baby could be born.

Theresa wanted to have the baby but was so miserable she couldn't plan the wedding. But when she emailed after years of silence, I was more than happy to help. Anything to get away from my house. Anything to get some space from Mother. Her sadness was overwhelming. Her sadness was an illusion. She'd pretend to be fine but then wash the same dish for twenty minutes.

My brother, Junior, didn't come home from university in Montreal for my father's funeral, but he called to say he'd be present for Theresa's wedding. My immediate family was small, so the day was filled with members of our community. They were family nonetheless: aunties, mammies, and uncles all dressed in the same fabric showed up at the house, though nobody had actually invited them.

Aunt Adele was incredibly stressed. But it was nice seeing Mother and her sister together. I thought that they could really help each other out during this time. Aunt Adele hadn't recently become a widow, but she still talked about her divorce as if it had happened yesterday. Aunt Adele asked me not to tell Mother about the baby. And then she asked me not to tell anyone about the baby.

Theresa had always wanted to be pregnant. She thought pregnancy might give her an escape. Like me, Theresa had taken on the role of mothering Aunt Adele after her father left. And though Mother didn't need any reminders, I still felt responsible for her well-being. I felt guilty for having moved on. I felt even worse because I knew how much I looked like him. But this weekend was about Theresa. This weekend was about making sure she'd get through it. All of it.

Theresa wore wax for the dote ceremony. The pregnancy was new, and the arranged marriage happened overnight, but it was possible to hide both.

Theresa's fiancé was accompanied by his uncle and his father. They brought drinks, uncooked goat, and money for Aunt Adele. "How many goats do you think she's worth," the ongoing joke went. "Twenty if she's still a virgin," I heard someone say. "Twenty-two if she knows how to cook," somebody else said. Then, the room got quiet. Normally, the ceremony was held underneath a tree, and normally the father of the bride hosted the event. But my family had given up on real tradition years ago. Instead, we were making things up as we went.

I spent the entire night telling Theresa that she was beautiful. And the entire night, Theresa and I thought of names for her unborn child.

Then, when it was time to dance, Mother and I sat on the balcony. We watched the party unveil itself.

Jugs of palm wine used to kick off the celebration, but the family seemed content with boxed merlot. After the presentation of gifts, the house filled with music. Mostly drumming, and the popular sounds of Franco Luambo, Papa Wemba, and Koffi Olomide.

Mother and I brought fish. And Junior stood in the corner with his new girlfriend he refused to introduce to anyone. Theresa's dad showed up eventually, got gloriously drunk, and announced that his daughter was in fact a whore. The music kept going. Some uncles and aunties came up to Mother with late condolences, which we accepted, as members of the bridal family. As women. Armed with our willingness to overcome this too.

Finally, I got Theresa alone.

"Tell me you brought goodies," she said.

"A whole bag," I told her.

"Shrooms?"

"And liquid G."

We called this her last supper. Though it would be by proxy.

"And you'll do whichever I want?"

"Yeah, but when did you even get into all this stuff?"

"I live in the middle of nowhere. There isn't much else to do."

I didn't say anything to that.

From the bag, Theresa picked blow. Which was good, because it was the only stuff I could actually stomach. We were sitting in her car parked inside the garage. She reached in the back seat and grabbed an envelope, handed it to me, and said, "I kept this—don't laugh. I'm not crazy."

I was in my feelings, so my mind went immediately to endings. This was her goodbye party. Inside was something I had written for Theresa, nearly a decade ago: a "How to Insert a Tampon" guide. I had learned this from somebody else and was so excited to share it with her.

"I'm giving it back to you because I want you to give it to my daughter, one day."

"It's a girl?"

"I think so. I'm just going to put that into the world and hope."

I had no words.

"If I just sniff the bag, will it affect the baby?" she said.

"No, I don't think so," I said.

Theresa took a deep breath. "Eight more months and I can drink. But you promise. After this line, you're done. No more."

"Yes," I said.

I could do it too. I could put it into the world and hope.

We seldom talked about this either, but it was there.

"Last line and last wish," I said.

"Kiss on it," Theresa said.

So we kissed. Which I know was an odd thing for cousins to do, but we weren't ordinary cousins. And these weren't ordinary circumstances. And there was a field filled with grown-ups who believed in an unknown God more than they believed in us. And we were alone now anyway, so if we wanted to fucking kiss, blood or not, we would kiss.

Because I had been sober since my father's funeral, one line was enough to keep me up. And good. I otherwise wouldn't have been good company. I otherwise wouldn't have been able to take Theresa dancing, just to confirm that it was true I was there. And it was true I was born. In this life, and in this moment, and all of it had been against my own will. But, hey, I was making it anyhow. And Theresa would make it too. And Mother.

I left with Mother when the party was over. It took her a while to get inside the house. She sat on the porch to pray first. In the time it took her to pray, I began to pack. I was putting things that mattered inside a duffle bag. I had no plan. I had no idea where I was going. But I knew it had to be away from here.

Mother was still outside when I was done packing. I sat with her on the porch. My heart was heavy. Everything about being next to her suddenly made me feel uncomfortable. It was like I was feeling years of oppression in that exact moment. I wanted to cry, but I had given up on tears. I wanted to fight, but I felt too weak.

So I just sat there. And I waited. I waited for the courage to go. I didn't know where I was going, but I knew it had to be away from there.

THE BOY FROM MY YOUTH

I left home with a duffle bag and no plan. I didn't have a place to go. Didn't have a place to sleep. It didn't matter. I did what I was taught to do: I survived. I found shelter inside of a boy. I had let him pop my cherry, so for a week I thought he owed me this much. He was all I had and there was no turning back. I was grateful he had taken me in. It became romantic because we were both lonely and miserable and young.

He lived in his parents' basement apartment in the Guildwood Estate. The floor spread vast and the ceiling hung high, and Dylan, at six feet tall, could stretch as wild and comfortable as he liked. I especially liked the marble floors, how the sunlight could pierce the long windows and reflect from the ground up.

A long wooden table took over most of the apartment. That was where he would study and I would read or write, and watch him. It would really just depend on the temperature and my mood. I felt most inspired after mid-night. Around the table were chairs, and then a sofa. So the open dining/ living concept made us feel quite domestic. There were exotic designs on the walls. Splashed colours of dirt or blood, the paintings were all bought by his father during trips to Thailand, South Africa, and India.

It was easy to fall in love with this new life.

In the morning I would make coffee. I could toast something French or fix an omelette to go along with the coffee. And I would usually have chicken simmering in the slow cooker by the time Dylan left for college. I loved this housewife role I had taken: I cleaned and did the laundry and rearranged the furniture until I found a set-up that would make Dylan feel more relaxed when he came home. He was studying to become an engineer. And when he wasn't spending all his money on leather, he was taking his grandmother out for lunch. His cleaning lady used to come down whenever she was done doing work for his dad, but after a month of living there, I told her she didn't need to. Cleaning was what I did to stay occupied. I would look for poetry inside an empty bag of Doritos, or a damp sponge.

We did a lot of lying around, and he would itsy bitsy spider up my back and go, "Ugh, you're just so ugh."

There was some truth to this—I had been made aware of it all my life. But still, I denied any suggestion that I was more than just regular pretty. Dylan told me I had a second and third puberty. The second one reserved for my breasts alone, the third for my nose, which, Dylan said, seemed to have shrunk over the years.

Dylan said I was the kind of girl that needed to be claimed immediately. Of course, I let him fuck me whenever he wanted because he was just so nice.

While Dylan was at school, I'd send him a series of nudes with my index finger sticking out of my mouth in every single one.

He'd send a series of texts back:

"Hot."

"ExXxtra good."

"Can you spread your ass cheeks in the next one?"

"Oh my god I can't wait to get home."

When he came home, we would jump right into it and give up after an hour. I didn't mind it one bit. He was honest while his head lay on my chest. He was most honest immediately after he came. He'd tell me his side of the story. His version of our childhood. He would tell me what it was like hanging out on Galloway, knowing that he had all the privilege of the bluff. In return, I would give him what he needed. The "You're Perfect for Me" and the "I Like You Just the Way You Are," as a way to regulate his serotonin levels. And Dylan would tell me that he was good, that he was the happiest he'd ever been, and I had much to do with it.

I figured this was better than sex—the real orgasm was the way he looked at me, from afar, from up close.

Still, there were things Dylan wished he could change about me: my toothbrush, my journals and books and papers. I couldn't bring myself to change, because he loved and worshipped my body. Dylan offered me this air of newness.

It was easy to fall in love with Dylan.

Calm, assertive, stable Dylan. And Guildwood offered the good and the hope and the light that co-op living couldn't. The real thrill of being with Dylan was that he always came home. I wasn't used to that growing up. I didn't have a routine or anything tangible to hold on to.

Then, Dylan came home one night and sat on the wooden table across from me. I had been working on petition letters to universities explaining the circumstances surrounding my poor grades in my final year of high school. I wrote about my mother becoming too depressed for me to handle, about my father's suicide, and about my brother Junior's need for space.

Dylan sat across from me. He rubbed his knuckles. "What are you working on?"

"A speech. A petition. A plea."

"Well, which one is it?"

"All of the above," I said.

"Can I do anything to help?"

"I have meatloaf in the microwave. And we should be good on laundry until at least Sunday."

I went back to my work. Dylan stared me down. "Is this what you do all day?" It came out softer than it was meant to.

"I also organized all the utensils with their own kind and by size."

I'm sure I said more things to impress him with my ability to be self-serving, self-sustained, self-entertained, self-motivated, and self-possessed. But still:

"This isn't working out," he told me.

I was still smiling, thinking of all my successes that day.

"Is it because of the sex?" I asked.

"What?"

"I don't make you come anymore."

"It's not that. I told you, I don't usually come anyways."

I straightened myself on the seat. Dylan told me everything so as to not hurt my feelings. Was it vulnerability that brought people together at the worst times, and so quickly? Or was it the rhetoric. Was it a miscommunication? A matter of translation? When he said, "It's not working out," was it the "it" part that was not working out, or was it the whole damn thing?

So I dug. Maybe growing up in a silent house had made me an expert at hearing the crack in things—the wall, the mattress, the kettle boiling dry. Maybe it was my need for proof of payment. I pushed and pushed and finally:

"I just never pictured myself with a black girl, you know?"

I didn't know.

He said more. *It's not you, it's me—well, it's a little bit you, but it's mostly me. I'm just not attracted to black women. But you, you were different. You were hurt, and you're like family. And, I don't know, you needed me, and I guess it was fun, at first, but then it got too real. And it's not that I don't love you, you must know, you're really such a lovable person.* And, and, and.

I didn't cry. Not because I didn't want to. But because this was Dylan. This was me. And by the time I was done packing, Dylan was broken. He was still going on about the sorrow. Still fitting me into his narrative. I sat next to him, brought his head to my chest, and let him sob. I imagined how strange it'd be if I just pulled out a nipple and let him suck on it. I rocked him until it hurt him less to leave me.

"Better?" I said.

"You're leaving?"

"Well, Dyl, yeah."

"You can stay until you find a place. You can at least stay the night. Or maybe you don't have to leave at all?"

I love this so much about men. How they can hate a woman and still want them. How they confuse fucking for an "I'll you see later."

"Dylan? I'm going to go now. Are you going to be okay?"

I had packed light, so I left light. My duffle bag was really just heavy because of the books. I got out into the night, and it felt freeing. That's the funny thing: Rocks lifting from your chest without you knowing they were there in the first place. The moon guiding a path without a pavement to walk on. I liked the night. I liked how it came at the end of every day, no matter what.

THE COMMON ROOM

BED FOR RENT. GIRL ONLY. EIGHTEEN OR IN THAT RANGE. MUST NOT BE SENSITIVE TO NOISE.

The ad on Kijiji read like a plot to traffic young girls. But I was desperate. And I was intrigued: bed for rent. Not room, not basement. It was located above a laundromat on Pharmacy and Danforth. I hadn't been this far west of Scarborough, but I recognized the smell: curry with a hint of feta cheese floating in the air. As for the sound: it was like playing music on train tracks.

"There's no bedroom?" I asked.

"Yeah, but everything's included," Olivia said.

"So what? We share a bed?"

"Temporarily, if you don't have your own, I guess."

"I don't know how comfortable that makes me."

"Everything's included, though. The hydro, the gas, the internet, all of that. Free laundry. And it's eight fifty. That's like, what, four hundred-ish each. You just won't find better than that."

I think we had most of the second floor to ourselves. If we had neighbours, I didn't see any. If the landlord lived on this floor, I didn't know of it. The apartment walls were red brick. The windows had classic, rustic frames and foggy glass. If you looked hard enough, you could see the bluff—it merged with the sky so that one could be confused for the other. The floors were hardwood, which gave the room this freshness. I had never occupied a space with hardwood. I had never had marble details on kitchen countertops. Olivia clapped her hands and the lights went off; another clap and they went back on. Whoever lived here before must have started renovations but gotten lazy. Probably couldn't be convinced of the value of this area—mostly crowded with bums and beggars, Toronto's traffic embedded in the makeup of the road.

I walked over to a window, and Olivia followed at my heels. "I'm doing an intensive interview. Just because I like you doesn't mean I'll pick you. Can't trust people from the internet and all that. But ideally, yeah, we'd share a bed and everything else. This woman, Alice, my mother, gave me all kinds of appliances and silverware, all that good stuff. We can also get a second bed. Like, I can get a second bed from Alice, that won't be an issue. It all could work."

"What if I wanted to have someone over?" I said.

"You should never fuck in your own bed anyway. But if it comes to it, we can always put up curtains. I could go out for a walk ... There's all kinds of shops around, the strip's not too far from here."

I moved in the same day. None of the questions she asked could exonerate me. None could confirm whether I was to be trusted. None could explain why she took an interest in me. They were a series of yes-or-no questions, none seemingly related: Do you like coffee? In the morning or at night? Do you have a specific television show you insist on watching live? How long do you shower, approximately? How necessary is solitude for you? What are your thoughts on *Les Misérables* as a musical and an honorary satire? On and on.

I arrived with a duffle bag and a box of used books. The books I had stolen from high school. I took all the ones we read and then some. It was my fuck you to the school board. It was my proof that I had been somewhere, and I that had left that place. I had nothing else. Just a couple pairs of pants, a few shirts. Exactly five pairs of underwear. One bra. I was really starting over. It felt liberating to part with my old clothes. My standard miniskirts and crop tops. My occasional boyfriend jeans. I brought with me only the necessities.

Olivia watched me move in my stuff. She was wearing blue overalls that had paint stains on them, though there weren't any signs of fresh paint anywhere. She had added to the apartment a grey sofa—a pullout, moreover—a brown coffee table, and a black carpet to make a designated living room area that faced the kitchen. There was nowhere to sit and dine traditionally. The bed was at the far end of the studio.

"You move light," she said.

"You decorated."

"They belong to Alice."

I had then only ideas of what the relationship between Olivia and her mother was like. I was comparing it to my relationship with Mother, but worse. Mother and I didn't hate each other. Nor did we owe each other any apologies. We were just not compatible. She would want the house to be set at a certain temperature, and I would have a problem with it. I would leave the door unlocked when I left for school or whatever, and she would have a problem with it. Those were the little things. Also, after my father's suicide, she lost her voice trying not to cry. We just mourned differently, you could say.

"Your mother sounds decent," I said, dropping my bag, kind of swaying my body back and forth as if to say, *What now?*

"Alice is a narcissist. Picture a woman having lunch somewhere in Yorkville, drinking mimosas with her girlfriends and saying, 'I bought Olly furniture from West Elm, ha, ha, ha, garçon, garçon, drinks on me today.'"

"She really fucked you up," I said.

"I'm amused. This is me being amused."

Olivia did this often. She told you who she was. She would laugh, this incredibly alluring laugh, and then she would confirm, "That was me laughing." This wasn't a flaw. I don't believe she had any real flaws. She was just sure. And in case you had her confused, she'd set you straight.

I went and sat down on the mattress. There was a brown dresser with six drawers on either side of the bed. I picked one at random and stored all my belongings. Afterwards, I sat on the bed unsure of what would happen next. I had the money from my father's will, but it wouldn't last. It would keep me for the rest of the summer. It would keep me until I turned eighteen and could find real employment. This is what I'd do until then. I'd sit and watch Olivia.

Behind the sofa she had created a sort of arts-and-crafts area. There still weren't any paints, but she had the look of a painter. She had the misery. She had crayons spread all around her. She sat on the bottom half of a wide sheet of paper about twenty by twenty. She coloured and I watched. Later, she sang, more like a robin than a human girl. I had never heard a robin sing, but I could imagine.

In the mornings, I'd wake and make us both a cup of coffee, and she'd settle down to draw. We got to know each other through that silence. I knew she'd sigh very heavily whenever she was at the height of a creative breakthrough. I knew she could only stay focused for about fifteen minutes or so, before she'd invite me to her corner for the distraction. She'd go on with her questions. None of which were personal. None of which were deep. But still, through that layer of superficiality, we were getting to know each other. *Do you like the colour red? What do you do when it starts to rain unexpectedly? What were your initial plans after graduation? Should I make the woman in this portrait yellow or violet?*

Most of her questions I could answer without a thought. But sometimes she'd stop me in my tracks.

"What's your best childhood memory?" she asked, and I went silent.

"Um. Immigrating," I said after a while. "I liked how my first experience in Canada was coloured falls."

"Have you ever been in love?"

Silence, silence, silence.

"I'm seventeen—what do I know about love?"

"Didn't you love your father? Or your mother? Were you sure of it? It's the same thing but with the added layer of loving to fuck them too."

"Well, I never really thought of fucking my parents."

I could always kill the conversation with such a response. She didn't push. She never dug to get an answer out of me. She understood her limits, and mine. If she felt that I was uncomfortable, she would drop the subject and resume her painting or her outlining. I really appreciated that about her. Though it often felt like the questions and the conversations were just a matter of filtering the silence. It was just a matter of hearing the sound of a human voice every so often, as opposed to the humming laundry machines downstairs, the honking of midday traffic, the yelling outside at midnight.

For the first month, I opted to sleep on the pullout and sometimes on the carpet until I could afford a bed of my own. Olivia didn't fuss, didn't argue, was very "do you" about it. She had the bed to herself. We ate on the floor, legs crossed, surrounded by pencils and pens, markers and paintbrushes. I didn't leave the apartment much. Only for groceries, which we did together. Sometimes I might leave to walk down the street and turn at the first sign of drama: a homeless person asking for a cigarette, a car honking at a pedestrian, the traffic light stuck on green. I felt suddenly overwhelmed by sound, by evidence of life being lived and unfolding.

The second month went the same, and in came August. I didn't tell Olivia of my new discomfort, but she knew. Somehow she always knew.

"I just worry you're turning into a hermit. I worry I did that to you," she said one morning.

"I'm just taking some time off."

"But it's your birthday. You can't just, like, not acknowledge it."

"I will—I'll celebrate it here. There's everything I need. Whipped cream in the fridge, and we can make a candle from a bamboo stick. You have so many, God knows why."

"We should have dinner. We should go drinking."

"And where would we find the money?"

"Alice," she said, after some time, as if for the first time.

Olivia and I had forgotten about the people we knew before each other. I hadn't heard of Alice in weeks, hadn't thought of Mother in months. We were concerned with the temperature of the apartment and the books we were reading. After that initial month, the conversations were usually like a book club meeting. Still with that same pizzazz of "Do you think Emma Bovary is a justifiable character?" Olivia went out a lot. She'd go to bars but would come home as if she had only been down the corridor and back. Nothing to tell. Nothing to report about the outside world. It was easier to believe it was just the two of us.

"Maybe I'll call my mother," I said.

"Maybe you should."

Instead, it was Olivia who called Alice. I couldn't hear what Alice was saying, but I heard Olivia ask for money: "Just a hundred dollars," she said. "Not for rent, Alice, for drinks. I gotta live my life too, you know." Alice agreed but said she'd deliver the money in person.

The money came, but there was no sign that Alice did. I had been home all day. Except when I went to shower, I had been watching the door closely, waiting. When Olivia began to dress, I asked about Alice.

"Your mother came?"

"I got the money," she said. She had bags underneath her eyes I hadn't noticed before.

"So, Alice was here?"

"Listen, put on the dress I got you, it cost me a fortune! Just get dressed and get a move on, man. You know, see things for yourself."

So I put on the dress and out we went. I got in the club with the same forged ID I'd been using for years. It was a picture of a light-skinned girl with big long curls, though I wore my hair short and straight.

"Just smile at the door," Olivia told me, and I did. I already knew to do this, but I almost needed her to tell me what to do. I smiled and smiled and smiled at the bouncer.

We ordered drinks at the bar, and then we looked around for anyone interesting. Or rather, I looked around while Olivia looked at me. A good thirty minutes went by and we ordered another round, and then a third. We waited until we were both feeling it to talk. It felt as if we were meeting each other for the first time. She seemed to me prettier, underneath the dimness of the bar. Her skin glistened. If you looked at her closely, you could see the glitter. It might have been literal. It might have been a residue of her day spent playing with shapes and textures and colours.

"I missed you," she told me when we were drunk, and I told her I missed her too.

It didn't make sense. We spent every single moment together, every day. But the fondness was there. Or the lack thereof was felt. There was this newness we had experienced when we first met that was gone. This excitement and electricity. There was this terrible feeling that we had experienced this great big love story and it was coming to an end, that we had been madly in love and then left each other for years, and now we were meeting again as new people. As the people we were meant to be all along.

"Tell me something I don't know," she said.

"My dad died, couple months ago."

"I know that—that's not new. Tell me something unexpected."

"Um. My mother got so depressed I moved out."

"No, that's too obvious. Really wow me. I want to start over. I want to get to know you. I went about it the wrong way."

Well, fuck, I thought. I was drunk. I was out. I was in a place I thought I'd never be, and I was looking at this girl and I was thinking, *She might be it*.

"I was relieved when he died. It felt like this huge rock I didn't even know I was carrying had suddenly lifted, just like, fucking flew out of my chest, you know? Like, no more suffering, no more hiding. Everyone free."

I said it and nothing happened. The roof of the bar didn't crack open, and no birds flew from heaven, and there was no earthquake. Olivia didn't offer me any condolences. She didn't tell me everything would be all right. She didn't look at me any different either. She ordered two more drinks and we cheersed. Whatever I said didn't lead to any psychoanalytic conversation. It was just put out into the world, and nobody died because of it.

By the end of the night, when the bar was closing and we had been on our feet dancing, I had forgotten what day it was. I had forgotten about everything in the world except what I knew: we were there, and now we were here, dancing.

When we got home I got in bed with Olivia. I wanted to kiss her, but I felt that kissing her could scare her away. She seemed like the type to run from affection. I wanted to lean forward and breathe the sweat from her forehead. I wanted to become one of her sweat glands—saucing down her face with freedom. I stared; she stared back. I'm not sure what time it was when we finally fell asleep, but in the morning, when I woke up, we were in that exact same position. She was blinking slowly, or still trying to fall asleep.

We went about our day the same as always. I cleaned. I rearranged the furniture. I sat on the mattress, reading. I joined Olivia on the floor when she asked me to, answered her Q & A on my food likings. I laughed and laughed, and everything in that laughter felt sweet.

Whenever she was in a different corner of the apartment, I missed her. When she went out, I missed her. I longed for her. I stood by the window and watched her cross the intersection. She didn't look before she went. She didn't wait her turn. She didn't wait for the traffic to slow down. She simply cut across the road, all certain, all unafraid, causing one car to swerve just a little and another to honk angrily. It was then I got the sense of who she really was. Fearless. Maybe reckless. Sad by omission. She went through life like someone who wanted to get hurt. When she reached the other side of the street, she kept on going—not once looking back, not slowing down. Unconcerned with the mess she left behind her: a man pulled over, one foot out the driver's side door, yelling, "You stupid fucking cunt!"

When Olivia got home late that night, later than usual, I was already in the bed. She got undressed and joined me. We lay face to face but without touching. She smelled of solvent and water, though still, I had yet to see paint around the house. She blew in my face, and that was enough: I crossed my legs and squeezed them together, and reached an orgasm. She did too, but still, no touch. No kiss. No nothing.

The next day, Olivia left early and didn't come home until late. Same thing. We lay in bed. No touch, no kiss, no nothing. This went on for a few nights until finally she came home, but with her was another girl.

"This is Anna," she told me. "My girlfriend."

I laughed. What else was there to do but laugh?

Olivia, Anna, and I sat in the living room. Each of us minding our own business. Underneath us, we heard the laundry machines humming. We had to be extremely quiet to hear it.

MEN, TRICKS, AND MONEY

"You have a nice pussy," Isabelle told me. "Can you start today?"

I worked at the spa for eight months. I worked there until I had made enough for university. Only a few of the girls who worked there were students. By the end of my run, it was only Lisa/Sugar and me. Then, it was just me. Some of the women were mothers, or had been married and then divorced, or were immigrants, or were running from domestic abuse. Most of the women just wanted to clear some debt. Most of them didn't even work there out of desperation. Most of them just wanted to fuck capitalism.

The afternoon I arrived for my interview, the sun came out to save me. I noticed a sign that said HOT GIRLS OWN HOUSES. The sign was glued to the darkened front windows. The interview was more like a casting couch. I walked around the lobby, took some clothes off, fondled my nipples, danced, and spread my legs. The lobby was clean like the foyer of one of those high-rise downtown condos. It had white marble floors, even whiter walls, dimmed low light for an intimate and cozy ambiance, one large yellow sofa. It was an island on its own. It was the thing that didn't belong but needed to exist for this place to stand still. It gave the feeling that you were entering a cave.

Two days later, I was done training. The job was only supposed to last a few weeks, but the money was exceptional, and there was Lisa/Sugar—a transactivist who knew every word to every single Bon Jovi song and every argument used to counter Darwin's theory of natural selection. She was impressive. She studied in between her clients and had permanently manicured fingernails.

Lisa/Sugar and I met up every evening at around six p.m., when we were both done the day shift. I still went days without eating. I still made difficult choices, like a spoonful of peanut butter or crackers and cheese. Wherever I was before this was such a bad place that I was afraid of being anywhere else but here. "Come, I'll buy you dinner," she'd say, and I'd know it was code for: *I'll buy you dinner, give you a place to shower. I'll fix my futon for you too.* Whenever I would leave behind $100 in her purse or underneath her bed, I'd later find it tucked inside my journal.

Whenever I told myself, *Tonight is my last shift*, I'd go see Lisa/Sugar, I'd stand in her studio apartment, I'd admire the art she hung, the hardwood floors, the workstation that overlooked downtown Toronto. This was usually enough to make me want to go back to work the next day.

"How'd you do it?" I asked.

Lisa/Sugar walked across the room and pressed a button. The blinds came down to cover the floor-to-ceiling windows. She looked so happy, knowing exactly what was hers and how to operate it.

"You can't get too in it—you have to go in, get what's yours, and then go home. Church and state. You just have to decide what's your church and what's your state. What's more important to you? The prayer or the god?"

That night, she told me she used to have dreams of being the first woman to walk on the moon. I listened to her stories like lullabies. She was from Guyana. She considered herself more of a therapist than a sex worker. She'd look at a tree and see it as shelter. She'd look at a bench and see it as a riding horse. Whenever we went for walks, she'd point to two parallel buildings and say, "Don't they look like sisters?" She had a habit of talking in metaphors. Whenever she left to go see a client, I'd worry about her, though she'd tell me not to, sprinkling her armpits with baby powder.

My first client had requested someone who was ebony, petite, and fit. He was naked when I walked in. He was sitting on the table, covering his penis with his hands. I knew what to do because I just did what made sense. The only thing I was taught during training was how to smell a cop. The rest was up to me. "Massage them like you'd massage your boyfriend," Lisa/Sugar had said. I had never really had a boyfriend. I had never had an anything, actually. The man didn't give me a legal name. He wished to be called Dark Lightning. In turn, I told him to call me Baby. He asked for full service, and I said no. He asked for a blow job without a condom, and I refused. I felt both weakened and empowered. I offered him a body slide, and he came on my feet.

It went like this every morning. The girls, Lisa/Sugar, and I would meet in the laundry room, where we would hear about each other's real lives while washing towels filled with come. That much load in one basket was enough to kill your nostrils. For the first few days, I thought I was constantly smelling acid. The mood and the stories only got sombre during the night shifts. We heard about assault so often it became as common as good morning. But it never happened in the spa. The room was ours, and we were equipped with buttons that could signal distress. We were actually safer working in a place where there were so many of us and only a few of them. But it was the knowing that we were opening ourselves to that possibility that made us so kind to each other. Every *good morning* sounded like *I'm here if you need me.*

Once, I walked into my session and didn't see the man's face right away. He was already stretched out on the massage table. I began by lowering the towel closest to his ass.

"You seem tense," I said.

"Yes, very tense," he said.

I used the bottom of my palms to penetrate his shoulders. "What are you looking for today?"

I was a natural at this. In fact, I even got aroused rather easily. Often, I felt myself enjoying the session more than my clients.

"I want you to work for me," he said after some time.

"I can do that. What would my job be?"

"I want you to work on my plantation," he said, which I was not expecting. I even came out of character momentarily. Then I remembered what Lisa/Sugar had said about this place being a fantasy and people coming here to get what they couldn't get elsewhere. "We're doing a public service," she had said, again with the metaphors.

"I want to see you get your hands dirty," he concluded.

I flipped him over and finished the job. He came, sticky, hot, rapid.

Another time, I let a guy massage me. He was a regular and always tipped. We were talking so much about his two girls who were studying at McMaster, I didn't even notice when his fingers went inside me.

"Oh," I said.

"Sorry ... Is that not allowed?"

I considered this long enough for it to become allowed. I was surprised to know that my body had successfully been detached from my mind. It felt like I was giving birth to a whole new person. One was called *body,* and the other was called *brain,* and they didn't necessarily interact or feel the same things.

"Tell me about your wife?" I asked, because he had been using the finger that had the wedding band.

"She's lovely, actually."

This was the first time I saw him light up. I worked on him weekly and he could never relax. We'd need to try different positions or go from the shower to the tub, just to get him comfortable. I internalized this and assumed I was doing it wrong. He'd say, "Shut up, you know you're perfect," and I'd look at him, feeling my age, wanting so badly to go home. He talked about his wife for the rest of the hour. They got married at Casa Loma. Her favourite colour was orange. Sometimes, she called in sick at work just to read a book. He talked and talked and talked. It was nice.

When I told Lisa/Sugar this story, she looked at me like I had done something wrong.

"We all know what goes on in those rooms," I said.

"That's the kind of shit that's gonna get you sick, and get us shut down," she said.

"It's not a big deal. Everyone does it."

"There's a difference between fucking for money and pretending you'll fuck for money."

"Where would you be working if you weren't working here?"

"McDonald's."

"Tell me that story again? About the time your mother dressed you as a ballerina."

I knew Lisa/Sugar was quitting to complete her master's away from the smell of used condoms, yet I felt cheated by her departure. Normally, when I knew somebody was about to leave, I distanced myself. I hated goodbyes. People walked out on me without warning so often that I had gotten used to living without them. They came with too much expectation. But in this case, the leaving didn't come with a permanence. I would always know where she lived. I would always know where she'd be working. I would always know how to find her.

On the night of Lisa/Sugar's last shift, I was so happy for her I nearly died. The night came. I stroked some cocks. I imagined my life if I were to become a dentist. The night passed. I walked out of the spa a bit disoriented. It had been months since I had done this walk alone.

THE WAITRESS

The first man was in his forties, a real silver fox and a true gentleman. I was nineteen. In being with me, he was paying some debt to himself. Repenting for a series of crimes he couldn't speak of. My guess was that he had a daughter my age he had refused to raise. He wouldn't touch me. Even if I begged. I once showed up drunk and stripped for him. He locked me in the guest bedroom and told me not to come out until I had sobered up. I fell asleep and woke up to breakfast in bed the next day.

There was the Asian man who told me he had jungle fever, which didn't even make sense. He would take me to the most expensive restaurants in the GTA and always booked at the Hilton. He had a bit of a foot fetish and liked to rub butter on my elbows. After I got accepted to university, I asked him if he'd pay my deposit and registration fee.

"What do I look like, stupid bitch? An ATM?" he said, cutting his steak with a bit more precision.

"Sorry, daddy, please forgive me."

He loved the coy. They all did. Afterwards, I couldn't sleep for a month, nervous, thinking I was fucking for free. But the etransfer came late in August. He bought me a computer that Christmas and then told me he couldn't see me anymore.

I swore I was done with this. I got settled into my waitressing gig. I was entering my second semester debt free and relatively comfortable.

I met my third and final client while waiting tables. She was a regular. Had blue hair with grey roots. She was in her fifties; I was twenty-one by then. She tipped all the girls well and was extra nice to the ones who hugged her after her meal. She came every Tuesday lunch. Ordered rare salmon. I don't remember how she got me in bed, but the transaction was clear from the beginning. In her home she treated me with the hatred allotted to her because she was paying. She was no longer the warm, assertive older woman I had respected. She was mean—nasty. And she made sure I felt it. She made me her doll, her maid, her nanny, and her cook. I told myself if she asked me to garden when summer came, I would kill her. It never came to that. Her children were toddlers. We would be up in the attic while they played house on the main floor. Once, we heard a big fall. It sounded like a fruit bowl or a skull cracking on the marble. She kept going. We parted gradually and with no hard feelings.

Then I was just a waitress. A waitress/student. I had fallen into a real routine, and a depression. A reasonable depression where I could still do the mundane: eat, sleep, stretch on occasion. But once I was in the routine, I couldn't get out.

One morning before my shift I made steak and potatoes and sat reading on the steps. I was living in a rooming house that overlooked the university where I studied English. It was white with Christmas lights year long. Along with the steak and the potatoes, I usually had wine, usually it was red, usually I drank it with two ice cubes, but that day, I had coffee. The day before had proven to be difficult, and the day before that had proven to be long, and the day before that had proven to be—a day.

On this particular morning, my coffee cooled quickly. I was distracted by the people walking on the sidewalk. They were mostly students, mostly freshmen, mostly grumpy about their circumstances. I thought about warning them, but I grew tired before I could.

After I finished my coffee I sat on the bus to read. I would have liked to have taken a taxi instead. I would have liked to have stayed home even more. I would have liked to have my hair up in a high ponytail. Instead, I had gotten out of bed, worn my hair down, gotten on the bus, sat between two large men. The larger of the two asked what I was reading.

I said, "A book."

"What kind of book?"

"The kind of book that I read."

"Why do you read this book?"

"Because I enjoy the book."

"Why do you enjoy the book?"

It went on like this until the smaller of the two said, "Let the woman read."

Unfortunately, the larger man did not let me read, which upset me to the point of tears. For the day, I had coffee instead of wine, wore my hair down instead of up, took the bus instead of a taxi, answered questions instead of asking them. Not vital things, but still—tears.

I took a moment to compose myself. I did not want anybody to see me this way. I did not want anybody to look at me and say, "What's the matter?" with so much pity I'd go off in tears again. I did not want to have to explain that I was not entirely sure what was the matter, but that the matter was here, and had been here the day before today, and the day before that.

Of course, a guy I had slept with by mistake came up and asked:

"What's the matter?"

"Nothing."

"Are you sure?"

"Absolutely."

Then a girl I was serving asked me if we had washrooms inside the building. I answered, "No. As an establishment," I said, "we don't believe in facilities."

Another asked, "How hot is your hot sauce?" I answered, "Hot."

Then some guy with a snaggletooth told me that I should really consider how I speak to people. I told him, "People should really consider how they respond to the way I speak." We agreed to give each other some space.

While we were giving each other some space, one of the waitresses came up. She asked me if I'd had a meal today. I told her I had made steak and potatoes. Bad coffee. She repeated herself:

"Yes, but did you eat?"

"No."

"Listen, kiddo, you've gotta eat."

She said this smiling very wide. Then she walked away to greet a table. I watched how she did this: used her right leg as a pivot point, held her shoulders pinned backwards, tilted her head slightly to the right, smiled, introduced herself, smiled some more. Next, the table was laughing, and she was laughing. Then she turned in my direction. For a moment, her face was blank, she blinked too slowly, as though to remind herself how to breathe, then she smiled again. The thing was permanently printed on her mouth. She entered the order into the computer, smiling.

I kept watching her. I kept thinking: *How does she do it?* And then, suddenly, that feeling transferred from server to server to server. We were all going through it. We all had lives outside of here, and we all came here to forget about them.

SHUT UP YOU'RE PRETTY

I felt inadequate with Patty. She was Ethiopian, studying international development and psychology. She knew so much about so much. She was born in Africa too, and had immigrated too, but kept in touch with the culture and the traditions and the people, and when she spoke about society, I knew she was responding to the differences between the West and the East.

I moved in with her in a rundown building near campus after my sophomore year in university. We sat on the balcony overlooking a traffic light that stayed red. We had been in the apartment for a month and hadn't seen any work being done, no traffic police, no crossing guard to decide the right-of-way. People knew when it was their turn to cross the intersection by instinct. The cars knew to slow down and wait for the kid with the basketball or the mother with the stroller, though nobody could predict which way they'd go. Nobody crashed. Nobody missed their turn—no pedestrian, no vehicle, no squirrel, no stray cat.

Patty said, "They're all connected," and I could tell by the way she said it—thinking of a theory—that she was practising for what she called "the real world."

When we went back inside, she drew a circle on the whiteboard in the living room and said, "All organisms are born with innate biological tendencies that help them survive. Basically, instinct drives behaviour, not need. It's like a dog shaking itself after it gets wet, a sea turtle seeking out the ocean after hatching, or a bird migrating before winter. You don't have to see a kid at the light to know that one might suddenly appear."

We sat on the balcony every night in case of a crash. That way we could pose as valuable witnesses. We'd have to tell the police how this part of Scarborough had been ignored, that the streetlight didn't always turn on and nobody shovelled the snow. That the building where we were living had outdated carpets, a dirty pool, elevators that got stuck between floors.

"Someone's going to have to get shot for the city to give a shit," she said.

I asked her about Jonas.

She looked at me and rested her weight on the table. Then she said, "He's a TA. He's out of the question."

"But he's not my TA—and he's graduating in, like, two months."

"Everyone wants Jonas," she said. "Even Jonas wants Jonas. You'll have to get in line behind the girls who have already fucked him, and all the psych majors. And, also, he thinks he's a philosopher. He thinks he's a spokesperson for, like, the brain." She told me there was a girl who changed majors twice, just to end up in his class, and then, when the course was over, she dropped out of school. "Nobody knew what happened between them, but assumptions were made." She raised a brow. "What does your gut tell you about that?"

"She realized school wasn't her thing?" I said.

"Really? You're going to put this on her?" she said.

"We're all connected right? If I changed programs so much, it wouldn't be for some dude. It'd be because nothing felt right."

"She left midway through last semester."

"It didn't feel right."

"He told her that he loved her, and that she should model," she said.

"And she believed him?"

"He's a PhD candidate."

At the intersection, cars drove slowly past. A bus unloaded a classroom of kids, seven or eight who could have all been related. They ran in every direction. Everyone waited.

"See?" Patty said. "Instinct."

I was standing in line at the Tim Hortons on campus when I saw Jonas. He was ordering, leaning forward over the counter and whispering his order to the cashier. She blushed, covered her mouth with her free hand. Her hat was red. If Patty were here, she would have said, "Women dressed in red are more sexually attractive to men." Jonas had a grin on his face. He went and leaned on the display, waiting.

The cashier said, "Next," and a boy—a maybe-freshman, seemingly uninterested—spoke quickly and then stood next to Jonas. The cashier didn't look up from the screen. I wondered if the maybe-freshmen also found her attractive. Her hair was hidden underneath her cap. She had an oval face—a chin that wanted to make a point. She had red lipstick and orangey freckles at her hairline. She didn't look at me either when it was my turn. She dropped my change on the counter, still fixated on her machine, and then yelled, "Next!"

I went and stood in front of Jonas.

"I know you from somewhere?" I heard him say.

The maybe-freshman and I both looked up over our shoulders. The maybe-freshman smiled just a little, like, *Are you talking to me?*

"Were you in my class? Last winter?" Jonas said.

"Yes," the maybe-freshman said eagerly. And "My roommate, Patty, was," I said, with the same enthusiasm.

Jonas laughed without moving his mouth or making a sound. He looked directly at me.

"You gave me a cigarette at the alumni mix and mingle last month," I continued. "We were working the bar."

"Ah," he said. Just then, order twelve was called. Jonas raised his coffee at me and walked out.

The maybe-freshman and I rocked our bodies silently. That was our second chance at a first impression, and we had both fucked it up.

When I got home, Patty was in a baby cobra position on the living room floor. She was wearing nude tights and a sports bra. She looked good in anything, but this particular look gave her body volume. For someone so intuitive, Patty never knew when I was looking at her. She never knew when I was pinching myself so as to not sound stupid around her. Sometimes I didn't know if it was Jonas I wanted or Patty. They both had a holier-than-thou attitude—it's just that Patty didn't know this about herself. I let her have it because there's so much beauty in oblivion.

Between inhales she told me that the first cup of coffee came from Ethiopia. That was her reaction when I told her about sharing a cosmic connection with Jonas.

"A baby goat nibbled on a fruit, and voilà! Coffee."

I built up the courage to ask Jonas out. It was mid-October and I knew he'd be coming to the pub for his department's Christmas party. I traded shifts with Patty just so I could be there. I wore bright red lipstick, though I felt self-conscious with such a poppy colour.

I just walked up to him and told him I'd be done my shift at nine.

He said, "I'll buy you a drink."

He asked again if we'd met before, and I understood this was a reverse-psychology thing designed to make me feel vulnerable. He took me to a bar in the Rouge area, where we could smoke near the Port Union waterfront. It was cold, breezy, and uncomfortable—another one of his tricks. I was wearing my work skirt and shirt with a pullover on top. Upon seeing me shiver, he unzipped his jacket, pulled me towards his chest, and held me there.

"Do people ever call you Lol," he asked, and I said, "Sometimes."

"You shouldn't let them," he told me. "Loli is such a fine name. Curious, even if you listen closely. Loli, Loli, Loli. You can hear the intentions in that name."

Jonas told me that in some religions, the ocean is female. It was the oldest, most alive, most beautiful woman he'd ever seen.

"Loli means sorrow," he said. "It derives from the name Dolores, made famous by Vladimir Nabokov."

"It's actually a stream back home," I said. "When my mother was trying to get pregnant, she threw in gold and wished upon the Loli River."

Jonas shushed me. It was then I realized we were dancing. The shushing took the form of a melody, and that was the rhythm to which we swayed.

We went hiking down the Altona Forest in Pickering. I asked if Patty could come, but Jonas said he didn't think it wise for him to interact with his students outside of campus. The way he said this made me believe even Patty belonged to him. She said that he would kidnap me and bury me in the woods.

"That's probably what he did to the other girl," she said.

I laughed but considered it—this was my life now. It had no true meaning. I spent my days watching people get from one end of the intersection to the other. The only relationships I had were the ones that ended before they started. But when Jonas asked, I caught a fly in my mouth, picked it out, and said, "My most recent was with a boy named Mr Fly. I ate him and he died. I didn't mean to, he just flew right in front of me."

Jonas didn't laugh. I didn't know that my intention was to make him laugh until he looked at me blankly instead and said, "Shut up," touched my chin, and moved my head to align with his. Studying the structure of my nose, he smiled and said, "You're so pretty."

After he kissed me, I pinched together my thumb, index, and middle fingers and said, "A little insecty but good," and then, finally—laughter.

Neither of us said anything the rest of the trail. I followed along behind him. Sometimes he would grab me by the hand and pull me forward so that our bodies could be linked shoulder to shoulder. He towered over me, so it was more like shoulder to elbow. And every time we'd swing together again, what I felt wasn't electricity but the opposite. Like fingers putting out a light.

At a café, we watched a couple of teenagers run out on their bills.

"Let's pay for it," I said to Jonas.

"Why?"

"I just feel bad. The owner might make the server take care of the difference."

"Maybe she should have been paying better attention."

I sipped my coffee. "It could have happened to anyone."

"Not to you," he said. "Nobody would walk out on you. I mean, look at you. It's all about presentation."

We went for another walk after dinner. This time, it was the bluff. I didn't relate to the attractiveness. It was, to me, just a field with sand and water, rocks and trees.

Jonas told me I needed to really open my eyes to see. He stood behind me, lifted my arms like an eagle, like we were Rose and Jack in *Titanic*, except onshore, and said, "Look—what do you see?"

I told him I saw water and the sky, and he said, "No, I need you to really look."

"I see Santa Claus, except he's made out of cotton candy."

In the car he kept one hand on the steering wheel and the other firmly on my thigh. He didn't smile, or grin, or look at all happy to be there. But his grip was tight, and hot. I couldn't wait to have sex with him. I couldn't wait to feel what Patty had previously called "extra connectiveness."

Jonas lived about twenty minutes out of Scarborough and swore that the difference was like two separate countries occupying the exact same soil.

I said, "Like two different cities, you mean?" and he said, "No, no, the differences are in the measure of extremes."

Jonas lay my body on his bed. He lay on top of me and began to thrust through the fabric of our clothes, like what we used to do in high school. He massaged the sides of my cheeks and murmured to himself, "So pretty," over and over again until he came inside his pants.

He told me that sex was an activity of the mind. He brought his forehead to my forehead and said, "Can you feel it, can you feel me fucking you."

I nodded.

He told me the strongest, most mature minds can reach the point of orgasm without touching. The most fruitful and wise minds can kill without meaning to.

Jonas graduated with high distinction in November. We had real sex for the first time, and when he came he whispered in my ear, "Fuck," so longingly, the word sounded like four syllables instead of one.

Patty was still in that cobra position when I walked in. Sometimes I wondered if that's how she stayed all the time. I would leave in the morning and come back late at night to see her unchanged. I mainly stayed with Jonas, but whenever I came back to the apartment, what made it feel like home was Patty, body lifting off from the ground. It was like a familiar smell. She was the smell. She was the home.

I stretched out next to Patty, pushing my chest into the carpet.

"People back home believe that yoga cures diseases," she told me.

"I think that's just people all over," I said.

"But there's modern-day medicine here. The degree of importance is different."

I arched my back and waited until my breathing could meet hers and we chorused our inhales. I missed her. I missed this. I shut my eyes as required for the healing, whatever that meant.

"I see Jonas has released you from his cage," she said.

"Don't be mean."

"Did you at least find out what happened to that girl?"

"I didn't ask."

Exhale, inhale.

"I think you just don't want to know," she said.

"It's in the past. It's not like I go around telling people I used to fuck for money."

Exhale.

"I didn't know that," she said.

I listened to her inhale, then I followed on cue. I was wearing jeans and felt the belt buckle dig into my stomach. I let go with a final exhale. "I guess that challenges your theories."

Later, in the kitchen, Patty apologized and said she just missed me, that was all. The switch happened instantaneously. The smallest reveal and she was looking at me like she was meeting me for the first time.

"Is there something wrong with my face?" I said, then brought a spoon to cover my left eye. "I see that tension is rising in you—should we return to the mats?"

Patty didn't smile, and I began to wonder if she knew more about Jonas than she let on. It scared me how quickly I went from feeling safe next to her to in need of shelter when she looked at me.

I stayed at the apartment while Patty went home for the holidays. Jonas was entertaining at his parents'—which was farther to the east. When he asked me if I wanted to come, I told him I preferred staying home and getting some writing done. Plus, I didn't know if we were together-together or just together, and the intimacy of Christmas made the not-knowing feel too intense.

On Christmas Eve, at midnight, Jonas showed up drunk. I didn't want to have sex because I didn't want to have anything, but Jonas insisted, and I was lonely.

After he finished, he rolled me over and said, "Thank you, baby, ho ho ho," and walked out.

The next day, I forgot it was Christmas until I got Patty's email. It was a picture of herself and her nephew with the caption: *Two smiles for Loli, she's been not naughty and ever so nice.*

Something softened in Jonas. We lay in bed all through New Year's. He poked my nose, then my cheeks, then my ears during the countdown. He told me about his mother, who was a journalist, and his father, who was a university professor. There was the pressure to measure up, he told me, and sometimes, when he got angry, he couldn't control himself. He hadn't had any blackouts in the last year, but sometimes, one just hit him.

Now, every time he spoke to me, I looked for the aggression in his voice. Wherever it was, it was hiding underneath the words, and the theories, and the thesis, and the patients, and the hours he spent in the lab. Now, I only saw him at midnight. He'd come in using the spare key and curl his body around mine. He was tired from the new job and the new hours, and he was possibly tired from the new me. I spent more time writing since that Christmas spark. I was working on a poem about a girl whose soul was found in a river, and the people who found the soul were cursed to spend the rest of their lives looking for the body. I couldn't think of a reason for the curse, and I couldn't think of a reason the people who found the body should be made to suffer. But I wanted the poem to work anyhow.

Jonas told me the poem needed a heartbeat. "Remove that first line—your enjambments are sporadic and unaccounted for. Actually, I think the poem needs a new poem." Jonas's solution was that I needed take time away from the work. As it currently stood, he told me, it had no meaning at all.

Maybe I was the angry one: I asked him what we were, and I knew that by asking, I would be hurting him. Still, I said, "Is there any meaning in us? When people ask me where I'm going, I tell them I'm going to see my question mark."

"Loli," he said, "don't do this. Don't put words in my mouth."

"I am doing the exact opposite of that."

"This is precious. What we have is precious. You're going to make it all complicated."

When we had sex that night, I wanted to. I thought it might make him stay a while longer. In the morning, when I woke up, I was alone again, and perhaps I had been alone all along. I heard Patty singing in the kitchen. It was a French song from a popular African fable. Patty didn't know a lick of French, but sometimes she'd pull a stunt like this if she felt I could use it.

I called Jonas, but the phone rang and rang. After reading week, I felt such a lack without him. Found that I was unable to study, unable to write or get excited about anything. And Patty had started seeing someone just as she had come back home. Now I felt the emptiness of the apartment, as if Patty had sold all the furniture—all the paintings, the whiteboard, the stove—in my absence. I called her and she was at a party with hew new beau, Eric.

"Is everything okay?"

"Just wanted to hear the sound of your voice."

"Well, hell-ooo," she said, stretching the word to reach me. "What's wrong?"

"Nothing."

"That doesn't seem right. You wouldn't be calling at two a.m. for nothing."

"I didn't notice the time."

"Okay, I'm coming home."

Before I could object, Patty hung up.

I was pretending to sleep when she got in bed with me. She dug her hands in a container of Vicks and rubbed it on my back. We did this whenever one of us was feeling homesick. I kept waiting for her to say I told you so. Instead, she ran her fingers across my belly.

I showed up at Jonas's unannounced. He didn't open the door when I knocked. I sat on the doorstep and waited. Twenty minutes later, Jonas opened the door. He said I knocked like someone who didn't want to be greeted. He said I walked into a room like someone who was trying to get out of one. He had grown a beard and was wearing PJs, which he had previously told me he didn't believe in.

"What is it, Loli?"

His hair was sticking out funny, and even though he was smiling, he didn't seem glad to see me. He walked to the kitchen, and I trailed along behind him.

The house seemed big and dark and formal. We leaned against the counter. I had a million things to say, but now, looking at him, nothing came out. I became afraid that if I even tried for words, sounds I never knew I could manage would gallop out of me.

Jonas leaned over and kissed me.

I turned my face to the front door down the hall. "I didn't come here for that," I told him.

He ran the palm of his right hand from my belly up. When he reached my chin, he scraped it, kindly. Jonas kissed me again and I shook my head to indicate that I did not want to be kissed. I just couldn't find the words to fill in the blank. He reached his free hand and unbuckled my pants. He placed a finger inside of me. And then another. And then, he squeezed a third in. His nails began scratching the inside of my cunt.

Jonas lit a cigarette after he came. I surrendered next to him. He was quiet. So was I.

He said, "What?" But before I could answer, he said, "You know what, I don't want to hear it."

I moved towards him to be held. I needed him to hold me more than I had ever needed to be held. When he didn't, I felt a big suction evacuate my stomach. I felt a sharp pinch on every corner of my body.

This was what I wanted. This was what I came here for. No, really.

I stayed with Jonas every day for a week. I missed a midterm, and then I missed a few lectures.

Every day, he would work from home and I would lie bodiless on his mattress. I don't remember if I ate. After he was done working, he would find me exactly as he had left me. He would undo his pants. Sometimes he'd masturbate while I just lay there. Once, when he got blind drunk, he stuffed butter inside of me. I think he thought it was a tub of coconut oil, which I usually left in the fridge. Either way.

I phoned Patty from Jonas's.

"Hello?" she said.

"Patty?"

"Is that you? Please come home. I'm worried. Should ... should I call your mother? I'm—"

I hung up after twelve seconds.

"You're hurting me. It hurts when you do that."

"Do you know what hurts?" he said, and punched the wall behind him. "Look, baby, at my knuckles."

They were fine. A little red but practically untouched. The wall was fine too.

"All right," he said, and walked out, slammed the front door. I was in a bra and underwear when I ran out behind him, headed in the opposite direction. It took me an hour to get home on foot, in flip-flops. While I was crossing the bridge between Pickering and Scarborough, a few drivers honked. Others yelled from their window, "Put some clothes on!" They were teenagers. I could tell by the squeak in their screams. It only occurred to me later that I would have liked to have been run over by any of those cars. I would have liked it if a driver had accidentally lost control of their vehicle. I walked home wondering if I would have instinctively dodged, or stopped, or run forward or backward if such a thing had occurred. The desire to kill myself via incoming traffic didn't feel real. It was like a concussion. It was like my body was a concussion.

Back at my apartment, I had laundry downstairs from last Friday. I rewashed it to get rid of the mildew smell. Threw in my pants and shirt too. I sat on top of the machine, my butt cheeks absorbing the cold. I couldn't locate myself in my skin. Couldn't figure out in which order to arrange the feelings I was feeling. A man walked in. I knew he could smell me from my week-old underwear. I couldn't even remember the last time I had showered. Either Thursday after yoga with Patty, or the day before that. The man kept looking at me curiously, and I wondered if I had suddenly become transparent and he could see my blood boiling, turning into thick glue.

"Would you like to fuck me?" I offered.

I followed him to his apartment. He removed the checkered shirt that made him look like a parody of a farm boy and offered it to me in the elevator.

He said, "I don't have to pay for this, right?"

I didn't feel any pain during the sex. I didn't feel anything at all. I moaned with an echo until moaning turned into a tearless sob, until a tearless sob turned into blinking eyes replaying it over and over again. The man let me shower in his apartment. I rinsed my mouth with salt and water, something people did back home when they didn't have anything else.

I came home dragging my clothes in my arms. Dropped them in the corridor to knock on the door, and when Patty opened it, I bent to pick them up again.

"What did he do to you?" Patty asked when she saw me.

"I missed you too, sweetheart."

I was wearing my most conservative black dress. Pink flip-flops. I had washed my hair with men's shampoo, and it smelled like ice. Patty hugged me for a long time, patted me everywhere as she did, as though to check if I had tiny bombs planted on my body.

While she put the kettle on, she told me she had been accepted to the same lab that gave Jonas his head start on his thesis. She was so content, and proud of herself, the way she stood next to the counter as though it were made out of gold. Everything she did was with grace. I imagined she'd mourn with grace. She'd say something like, "Let's not cry for the person we've lost, but let's celebrate the life they lived." Nobody had died, but still.

For dinner, we had pan-fried fish wrapped in pita bread, with a side of garlic yogurt. A recipe Patty had picked up while home for the holidays.

"Did you say your mom owned a breakfast place, or?"

"That's my dad," she said. "My mom's a seamstress. It's all the same thing, though. Cooking, sewing. Anything with your hands, really."

"Like painting," I said.

"Yes," Patty said and smiled. "Everybody at the bar misses you."

"What does that even mean? Everybody and misses. Misses what. They don't even know me."

I realized that was true for Patty and me. Did we know each other? Or were we only aware of each other's habits? She sang when it rained, and she sang when what she really wanted to do was diagnose me. She sang to study my reaction to her singing. So much about who I was she had guessed by observation. *It's all connected*, I thought. Even the way she comes and opens my curtains in the morning. It's all the same.

"How do you feel about going to the hospital with me?" I said.

"To do what? Visit the sperm bank?"

"I don't know—just 'cause."

Patty and I lay on the sofa. She combed my hair with her fingers. She curled the baby hairs at my hairline and said, "This little piggy went to market. This little piggy had roast beef. This little piggy had none. This little piggy cried, wee, wee, wee."

I repeated, "Wee, wee, wee," after her. I was laughing. So was the song. So was Patty. I could not have said why. There was just something so funny about childhood—how it attempts to prepare you for the slaughter. How it fails—how it is decorated like a nursery.

I stopped getting out of bed, and it was April. It had been a month since I had attended my last lecture. And the email from the TAs and the professors confirmed I was failing with no chance of redemption.

"You could go in and talk to the registrar," Patty said. She dropped a tray of raisins, milk, and yogurt on my bedside table. She popped a finger in my mouth and said, "You have to take this," referring to the antidepressants she made sure I got prescribed. At first, Patty would crush the medication into tea or water to make sure I was actually taking it. I knew what she was up to, but I was so weak I didn't have the energy to object. "Maybe you can write an essay saying you got sick and couldn't attend class—I could write it for you." She picked up the clothes I had lying around the bed. Some underwear and stockings.

"I was thinking maybe we could go to Health and Wellness sometime this week. They have a pretty good group of people you could talk to."

"You mean therapy," I said, the words sticking in my throat.

"Yes."

"They'll open me up and fill my brain with gasoline!"

I never made it to therapy. But seeing Patty in pain in proximity to my pain made the pain feel less like pain and more like a punishment I was inflicting on her. As if her presence in my life angered me and I wanted to give her a reason to walk away. I wanted to push her off the balcony, during one of those mornings when we sat and watched the intersection. I didn't have the energy to tell her that it wasn't her constant care, or the medication, that finally got me out of bed.

I started by just showering in the morning. It was a small but tedious task. And then I was brushing my teeth and fixing my hair. One night, I looked into one of her African cookbooks and decided to make her a stew. I couldn't figure out any of the ingredients, so I phoned her mother in Ethiopia. She picked up after the first ring. I only inhaled and she knew it was me.

"I know how Patty sounds when she's nervous. She has the lungs of a whale," she said. The phone call lasted two hours. By the end of it, I had cried and I had laughed and I had burnt most of the stew, which, she reassured me, was normal the first time. "You've got to have a sense of the temperature," she said. "It takes practice." She told me that Patty used to want to be a nurse but was afraid she wouldn't be able to help as many people nursing and decided to study medicine instead. She had to beg Patty to agree to study abroad, she told me. Patty didn't want to leave her.

When she asked about my mother, it stopped me in my tracks. I'd forgotten I had one.

"Should I call her?" I asked a woman I had never met.

I couldn't stop writing. By the end of that school year, I had written seven versions of the soul, no body poem. I wondered, briefly, if this was what Patty meant by instinct.

Whenever I looked at Patty, I hated myself. She was such a sponge. She was such a reactionist. Sometimes I was mad at the mere thought of her. I often wanted to hurt her. I often wanted to shake her and say, "Let me out. Get out, get out."

This was my practice now: Patty would come home after a shift at the bar, and I would say, "Honey, I'm home," though it didn't belong in this context.

I would be in the cobra position when Patty got home. I even wore a pair of those nude tights that made her look her best.

"Is it my birthday?" she said when she walked in.

I smiled and said, "Maybe."

Inhale, inhale, inhale.

Patty stretched out next to me. "It smells like pork chops."

"I made stew."

"You didn't!" She gasped. And then a big exhale.

"I enrolled in summer school too."

"Shut up!" she said, and I resisted the urge to die, right then and there.

She came out of her cobra pose and tickled me, as if we were two little girls playing an interactive version of tic-tac-toe. We went to sit on the balcony, and I noticed that nothing had changed. The traffic light was still broken. The yellow school bus still unloaded the same kids. Cars still slowed by instinct.

A few days later, I was looking out at my neighbourhood from the balcony and puked. The vomit seemed to tighten as it flew out of me and hit the pavement below. I knew I was pregnant.

I went inside and called Jonas twenty-seven times. For what? I had nothing to say. I had no further questions. But I couldn't stop calling. I wanted to hear his voice. I wanted to hear his breathing. Then I would know for sure that I shouldn't have the baby. I already knew I shouldn't have the baby. I had never wanted a baby. It just felt wrong to make a decision for two people, alone. I hadn't taken a pregnancy test yet, but I knew. I knew in such a way that made me wonder if I had done it on purpose. For a solid ten minutes, I hated myself.

Was there a way to say, "I would kill for you," without sounding erratic? I asked Patty. She told me obsessive calling was enough to *make* me erratic. She warned: obsessive calling was the same as murder. You can go to jail for that.

By the tenth call, she threw a pillow at me.

I corrected her, "Do you mean obsessive calling is the same as suicide?"

"Yes," she said. "Social suicide."

She told me it killed her to see me in pain.

I wasn't in pain. I was in shock.

I went out for a smoke. It occurred to me that if I smoked all of my cigarettes, I would have a sick baby. I would have a sick bastard baby. I would have a reason to feel removed from the baby, other than the fact that I was its mother.

I said, "Hypothetically speaking, how long should I wait to call him again?"

"Never? How long is never? Because never."

"But hypothetically speaking."

"To say what?"

"I don't know."

"He'll think you're crazy."

"What if I had caught an STI, or got pregnant. Could I call him then?"

"Absolutely fucking not. He'll think you're making it up."

"In which case I would be crazy and a liar?"

"Exactly. Stop calling him."

I went to the park to get away from Patty. It was neatly tucked away inside a neighbourhood on Morningside, up the street from campus. Normally, I wouldn't go to a school park during school hours, but this was urgent. I wanted to see what happened to a baby after it had been born, and then raised, and then given a place to run around. It was cold. I could see my breath in front of me. It felt minty. I read somewhere, when I was five years old, that odd smells, odd tastes are the first signs of pregnancy.

The signs were there. My breasts were larger. But not fashionably. Swollen. Injected. If you listen closely, you can hear your body talking to you. It will tell you what it wants. It will tell you what it feels. It will tell you when it's being invaded. That's how women distinguish sex from rape, even if they don't know that's what they're doing. The body does. I remember reading something else, age fifteen: *The strongest women are the ones who listen to their bodies.* Was I a strong woman? Yes. I could feel the little tug, tug, tug. It was an imaginary tug, but it was the tug of my body telling me that something was inside of it.

Patty claimed my mood swings and my sudden inability to sleep were because of the withdrawal. "You are coming down from the greatest love of your life. Of course, you want to die. Of course, you can't sleep. There's a bit of a disturbance in being left, don't you think? Being left. It's like, one moment we're fine, and then the next, we're falling apart and there's just no easing into it."

Was it the greatest love of my life, or was it just the one that I had?

At the park, I watched one little boy holding hands with another little boy. They had no idea that people might judge them for the gesture. They held hands and they skipped, running around the park like two little lovebirds. The body doesn't know that a held hand can mean much more than that. Only the mind knows such things. The mind is the greatest nemesis of the body. And there, the tug in my body went again. Upon seeing more children appear outside the building.

Last night, for example, I wasn't dreaming, but a scene was unfolding before me while I was showering. A woman drowning a baby in a tub. That was another tug. Listen and you'll feel it. Tug, tug, tug.

The two little boys picked up sand from the sandbox. They showed no signs of wanting to leave each other. Maybe that was their bodies telling them that this moment wasn't going to last. Surely, neither one of those boys was thinking of what it meant to hold somebody the way they were holding each other. Yet here they were.

The sky was grey. And if this were another life, and if I were another woman, I would call for rain. But I was stronger than that. I knew the mechanics of my body. I understood the chemicals in the sky. I knew that a grey sky was not definitive.

My friend Rita had an abortion. It was the single most traumatizing thing that had ever happened to her. She cried every day after and talked about it non-stop. She would excuse herself while a group of us were having dinner to call somebody. And after she was done, she would hang up and call somebody else. She might call five or seven people before she joined us again. Her food cold. The bill already there. Her eyes would be filled with leftover tears. That was her body's way of telling her she needed to rest, to heal, or whatever it was people needed to do in such circumstances. But Rita wouldn't listen.

I didn't want to be like Rita

So I left the park. I wanted to know how the story would end for the boys. Would kids pick on them for holding hands? Would one of them trip and hurt himself? Would they miss each other if one of them moved away, or died? Would nothing at all go wrong? I was imagining one of those boys, or both of those boys, as my child. Already. Like that. Like magic. Never in my life before that day could I ever look at a child and picture it as my own. I remembered reading something else: *Motherhood begins at the moment of implantation. Motherhood doesn't end when a child dies.*

I went to Shoppers and scanned the family planning section. Condoms, pregnancy tests, cock rings. I took one of each. These were the ingredients for making a family, and I was with child. I couldn't decide if the cock ring was meant to go underneath the condom or on top of it. The cashier looked so embarrassed. I wanted to hug her. I wanted to let her know that it happens to the best of us.

Her thin lips were saying, "Fun night ahead?" so I said, "Yes, indeed."

The walk home was slow. Air, too much air. Every single time I walked home, I thought about how badly I wanted to leave the city. This city of air. My building was so poor-looking, yet a bunch of children were being raised moderately happy. The smell of piss started at the intersection. It combined with the smell of dog shit from north of Military Trail. When it was hot, when there were bees, the smell of gasoline took over.

Patty was in the living room. I didn't want her to see what I had in my bag.

"I'm going to call him one more time. And then it's done," I said.

"One more time, and then it's done."

It didn't ring this time. It just went straight to voice mail. And then it was static. And then it was dead. Being blocked is the same as being poisoned. It's like having a plastic bag wrapped around your head.

Patty did not say I told you so. Her face said, *Come here*, as though I were a child. And perhaps the real drama, the radical, the unbelievable, was that I was. I pouted. I obeyed. Then I locked myself in the bathroom. She followed at my heels. She didn't ask any questions. She just followed. I would have preferred her in the living room. Doing that fucking yoga she does at six p.m. every weeknight. Cooking something that could take the smell of everything else away. Something hot. Spicy and thick.

I stayed on the bathroom floor for a few hours after I got the confirmation. It felt like a wasteful day. When I came out, Patty was sitting on the floor in front of the bathroom. She had set herself up with her laptop and textbooks. She was working on a paper. She didn't ask me if I was okay, and she didn't ask me if I would be. She just looked up from the computer, and I crawled back onto the floor and sat next to her.

"Bad things happen to good people and nobody knows why," Patty told me.

"Jonas says that bad things happen to people who look like me," I told Patty.

Neither one of us believed this to be true. But this was my moment of vulnerability, and Patty was letting me have it.

WOMEN TALKING

The morning of the abortion, I ate a full meal. I didn't do it on purpose. I got distracted sitting on my balcony, watching a bunch of kids load into a yellow school bus. The scene was fascinating because each kid was the exact same height, but each looked to be a different age from the others. I kept watching the kids and eating the bagel. I was supposed to only nibble a little. Lick for flavour.

A woman sat down next to me at the clinic. She wore a red dress. Sunny and light. Her dress felt out of place. Inappropriately gleeful. She kept looking at me hard, or I was looking at her with judgment.

"I have my nephew's birthday party after this," she offered.

"Sure," I answered lazily. "After this?"

"I have counselling."

"Oh? They offer counselling here? I guess that makes sense."

"Yeah, she's great. Experimental. She's really big on removing words like 'crazy' and 'manic' from vocabulary about women. Why are you here? If you don't mind me asking."

"Abortion."

"Right. That was too personal. Sorry, I shouldn't have asked."

"It's fine. People get abortions all the time."

"You mean women? Women get them all the time."

"Women, little girls, whatever."

We sat silently for a while. Then, "You're really good at this," she told me.

"Good at getting an abortion?"

"You're just confident, you know? Sure of your decision."

I contemplated this for some time. "Well," I began, "my ex kind of raped me, so. Pick your battles."

"How does one 'kind of' rape someone?"

"That is a very good question," I said.

I turned my body to face the woman. She was beautiful and extremely young, maybe eighteen. She had strong shoulders and a prominent collarbone. She was built like an athlete, but her face was the contradiction. She turned to face me too. We sat in silence.

She told me her name was Steph.

"What an interesting way of saying that," Steph said.

"Saying what?" I asked.

"Abort. Like, abort mission. Like you had planned this entire life, and now you're like, never mind!"

"It's possible that some women have abortions and it isn't sad. It isn't the worst thing that happened to them."

"I guess that's very possible," Steph said.

The nurse walked into the waiting room and called for a girl named Tatiana. She was sitting a few rows ahead of us. She got up, and so did the man beside her. They hugged and kissed, void of emotion. I looked at Steph and she rolled her eyes, and then we both grimaced with our heads down. When the nurse scanned the room, it was like a teacher looking out into a classroom for the troublemakers. She led Tatiana by the small of her back. They disappeared down the hall.

"So my boyfriend thinks I have borderline personality disorder," Steph told me.

"Does he hate women?" I ask.

"It might just be me that he hates."

We laughed.

"Pretty much all the guys I've dated have called me crazy," Steph added. "The last one was a musician. He played guitar for a band called Smooth Sixty-Nine. And got all sentimental because I agreed to, like, sleep with the lead singer and stuff, and yeah. The whole thing was his idea. But intense sexual desire is a sign of, like, borderline."

"My roommate is a psych major."

"That must be really awful," Steph said, and I could tell she meant it.

"It's so bad that I didn't even tell her I was coming here today."

"You're better off that way."

More silence. This time, for ten minutes.

Tatiana came back. The man who was waiting for her grabbed her by the hand while carrying her purse in his other hand. He was tough-looking, with an unkempt beard. Tatiana limped. They left down the hallway towards the exit. What happened once they got outside was anyone's guess.

"That was definitely not an abortion," Steph said.

"Yeah, way too fast."

"That one's probably, like, STI testing."

"She definitely walked like she had herpes."

More laughter.

The waiting room was hot.

The nurse came back and called an Elizabeth O'Neil. She looked about sixteen. The woman sitting next to her was no doubt her mother. They were both in long black maxi dresses, both with orange freckles on their faces. The woman didn't move from her seat. She was reading a book and half pretended not to have heard Elizabeth's name get called. Elizabeth looked over to the woman, waiting for an order, or permission. But the woman continued to ignore her, and soon enough, Elizabeth left with the nurse.

"Oh my god!" Steph whispered. "That is a fucking forced abortion."

"No way. She's too far in the pregnancy. That is a standard check-up, and mama bear is pissed."

Now that Elizabeth was gone, the woman put the book away and began to cry. She got up and left.

"I've been thinking of shaving my head," Steph said after some time.

"What's stopping you?"

"Everyone. My shrink, specifically."

"Why do you want to do it?"

"That's the thing, I don't have a reason. I mean, do we need a reason for everything?"

"For most things, but shaving your head is really not a big deal. I did it once!"

"There's a cultural importance to it."

"What do you mean?"

"People are afraid of bald women."

I thought about this for a very long time.

"Do you have to have a reason for not wanting a baby?" Steph said.

"It's just not what I want, you know?"

"I don't have to have a reason to go bald."

"You just want to prove to everyone that you're exactly as crazy as they say you are." I said. "But listen, if it makes you happy, I think you should do it."

Steph ran her ran her fingers through her hair. There was nothing more to say.

The nurse came back and called my name. I had nearly forgotten why I was even there.

After the abortion, my life resumed as normal. There was a bit of discomfort as the local anaesthesia faded, but the discomfort felt the same as always.

OLD-FASHIONEDS

Ben stood with his hands on either side of his love handles. I peered from underneath the covers. He had a great-shaped chin. A narrow nose to match.

"Why are pouting? Come here."

"I don't know, boobs," I said, feeling like I had suddenly been stripped of all my clothes.

The first time we had sex, he cried after he came. I had never witnessed anything like it. He sobbed into the pillow, his neck getting redder as he breathed in intervals. I got out of the bed and reached for my skirt and my shirt and my shoes. He was supposed to be a one-night stand.

"You don't have to rush off," he told me.

"This was a mistake," I said.

"Please."

No one had ever begged me to stay, so I pulled my skirt off and crawled back into the bed. I held him between my breasts until he was fine enough to go again. We went for a second time. Then we sat in silence on his balcony. His apartment was on the twenty-ninth floor, overlooking the 401. We shared a glass of bourbon. Watched the cars on the highway. This was the part of Scarborough that turned into Toronto. And the people who lived in this specific building seemed equally in between two identities.

It was late at night or early in the morning. We finished the glass, and he poured another one. I was too drunk to keep going. I stumbled to his bed, not exactly sure if he followed behind. When I woke in the morning, he was already gone. A minute later, I found him in the kitchen making eggs. I was surprised at how relieved I was to find him there.

Ben went around the apartment slowly. He mixed bourbon and apple juice and slid the glass across the kitchen island. I was madly in love with that kitchen island. I always wanted one growing up, but we were poor. I fingered the marble top. It did not fit in. The rest of the apartment was trashed. The walls were an ugly red. The coffee table was a suitcase. The plants were plastic or dead. I lit a candle to mask the smell of the eggs.

"Lavender—how manly."

"Yeah? I have a whole box of unopened vanilla."

"So metro," I said.

"Does that turn you on? Because I have mint too. That's my favourite scent."

"The lavender is good. It fits the whole feng shui you've got going on."

"Most of the furniture is from my mom. Some I got at garage sales."

"The suitcases?"

"My father's. He's dead."

"How did he die?"

"Cancer," he said.

"Nice," I said. "Mine was a suicide."

He flipped the egg onto a plate. Then tossed it in the garbage as if he only now heard me. "You know what?" he said. "I'm a terrible cook anyway."

So we skipped breakfast.

He poured me another glass of morning apple-bourbon. We walked the dog. We shower-sexed. We stretched out on the sofa. I wrote him a poem. He sat up on the bed and listened to me read. Every day felt quite the same. We'd fuck. We'd drink. We'd eat. We'd say something we'd wish we hadn't. We'd walk the dog. We'd apologize. I'd read to him out loud. In that exact order.

"How many drinks have you had?" I asked.

"I don't know. Three, or five."

"Which one is it? Three? Or five?"

He leaned in for a kiss. The kiss was wet and long. If I hadn't pulled away, the kiss wouldn't have ended.

We crossed the road. The dog took a shit. She looked back at us and swung her tongue. He told me the funniest things she'd ever done: she ran away from a snowman last winter, she hid inside the laundry basket to challenge him to a game of hide-and-seek, she can smell me coming from the elevator, she wiggles her tail like a doorbell. I let him talk at me, and I let him kiss me. The talking and the kissing and the walking of the dog kept me coming back. The bourbon. The world I had outside of him was bad. It was winter now. The snow was uneven.

In the kitchen, he told me about work. Same old. Someone in the office pissed him off. He drank too much during lunch and never went back. Came home. Mixed himself a drink. Got in bed, and now here we are.

"You?"

"Uneventful."

"I'm going to make you an old-fashioned."

"I'm fine."

"You seem thirsty to me."

Now I was looking at him from the other side of the island, his brows together and his lips softened. He licked them and pressed them towards me. I got off the stool, and I began with my sweater. Then I fumbled my pants until I was out and he was in.

The sex was interchangeable. We used it as a home and a weapon. Otherwise, we fucked because it rained a lot on that particular day, and neither one of us liked it when it rained. By month three, the sex became troubling. I couldn't tell if we were having sex to feel closer to each other or to create some distance between us.

Later, we stretched out on the bed.

"Do I make your pussy squeamish?" he asked.

"That's an odd thing to ask post-sex."

"Tell me."

"Yes."

"You're the best girl I've ever been with."

"You haven't defined the relationship."

"We're here together. What more is there to define."

Ben rolled me over. He went in a second time. I felt better after we finished. We went out for dinner and shared a bottle of wine. He looked around, as though trying to catch a fly I couldn't see. He reminded me of a child lost in a parking garage.

"I don't know if people are looking at us because you're black or because you're beautiful or because you're with someone like me."

"Someone like you?"

"I'm old and miserable."

"I feel like men are more concerned with aging than women."

"You're youthful. You're the most exciting thing that's ever happened to me."

"Is that what I am?"

"You're the girl I've always dreamt of."

Ben was unhappy and I didn't know why. He hadn't experienced anything particularly difficult. His unhappiness was solicited. He walked around with a sign that said: *Nobody has ever shown me love. I have never shown anybody love.*

"I want to be more than that."

"No, you don't. I'm fucked up."

"This again."

"You deserve better than me. You don't know what you're talking about."

The waiter asked if we wanted another round. We had moved on to old-fashioneds. Without looking away from me he said, "Yes, keep them coming."

One night, I wiped him off my breasts. He leaned forward and took a swig of the bourbon.

"Are you okay?"

"I was just thinking—Jonas never wanted me to stay after sex."

"Your ex?"

"Yeah."

"What happened?"

"He was aggressive. And I don't know. Everyone after him had a girlfriend."

"It's because you're so fun, you know. I just want to put you in my pocket and keep you there."

"I'm that fun, eh?"

"Every time I look at you, I think, *Is she crazy? Why is she with me.* I don't get it."

"Jonas was an asshole, Ben."

"He probably just didn't know how to be with you."

"He used to call me crazy because I called him too many times."

Ben was now giving me his back. I still felt the pain of the sex. Or rather the distance of the sex. Or rather the fear that the sex was all we had. Or rather the feeling that the sex was all he wanted. Or rather the knowing that the sex was what kept us together. So I wrapped my legs around his waist. I nibbled on his ear.

"I get all weird and you don't judge me for it."

"I'm mostly weird."

"You know what I mean."

Often, I sat on the kitchen island trying another poem. He'd stretch out on the living room floor, pushing his face into the wood, as though to escape through it. I wouldn't hear from him for days, and when I did, he'd tell me another story: he couldn't get out of bed, his manager pissed him off, his mother was hovering. As for me, I had been reporting an intense feeling of suffocation. In that, my emotions were coming out of my body. In that, they were taking the form of people I knew.

"Do you mind if I sleep over tonight? I'm tired, and it's late."

"I don't think that's a good idea. If France shows up."

"And what if she does?"

"She's my girlfriend, Lo."

"Then why the fuck am I here?"

He didn't answer. I got up and got dressed.

"Am I your mistress or your whore?"

"You're being dramatic."

I walked out of the bedroom. Behind me, I heard him shout: "It's not that simple!"

"That's what you said six months ago," I shouted back and left.

This time, the breakup lasted two weeks. It was the longest we had been apart since we started. I don't know why I stayed. And I certainly don't know why I kept going back. Perhaps because I was so used to being there. So used to being that person. I could barely imagine it any other way. I was always the whore. I was always the mistress. I was always the one they reached for when they needed a drink. And maybe, after years of this, I was ready to accept it.

And then we were eating pizza and wings in his kitchen. Every so often, I'd look up to see if he had grown a new freckle on his face. He told me to stop staring. He told me a story about how his boss did not want to get married, but he had accidentally proposed, and now he was getting married. We laughed and we laughed. This is how we started, I suppose. We could not stop laughing.

"You have to boil the water first," he said. "Then add the sugar, then let it sit in the fridge."

We were debating how to make a good sour old-fashioned.

"What about the lime juice? The lemon?"

"That's not the point. You have to start with the basics. To build a house, you start from the ground. If the ground isn't stable, then the house will fall apart. Don't you agree?" he said, his teeth white as dry-cleaned bedsheets.

His apartment was cold. He did not grow up with heat in the house, and that was the one thing he kept from his childhood. We kept drinking the old-fashioneds to stay warm. The wall behind him took me in. It was a deep burgundy. The fridge was covered with pictures of him and France, on Valentine's Day, Christmas, and their anniversary last year, the year before that, the year before that.

"Is a house really a house without any windows? Floors? Bathrooms. A kitchen?" I asked him now.

He listened and took a sip. He had been tossing the bourbon around the glass in a circular motion. I was sitting in front of him on the island. He brought the tumbler to my mouth, then he drank his turn. He pulled me in by the hip, nibbled on my ear, bit my neck, whispered, "The foundation of anything worth having depends on how well you boil it."

He came in closer, then grabbed me by the hair, said, "Who's my naughty girl?"

I sucked on the old-fashioned. He laughed. I told him I didn't want any more to drink, that we should call it a night. He was a thirty-five-year-old senior manager at an electrical firm, something he complained on and on about. He said he did not have any purpose, that I should keep writing. That he should keep drinking. We had been at it for months and this was how we got along. He would read my stories and email back to say, "You're amazing." He had reached the peak of his career. I was twenty-six. France was also twenty-six. She was twenty-two when they started dating. But I was, he told me, his dream girl in the flesh.

He unbuttoned his shirt, picked me up, threw me over his shoulder, gave my ass a smack, tossed me onto the bed. He used to be smaller. Had lost all that weight from feeling small, from being in a bad place with France, from life running away from him, he'd explained. He looked healthier now, though he drank more than either one of us cared to admit.

When he left to take a shower, I noticed the self-help book I bought for him for his thirty-fifth birthday. The turning year. The year all men live to die. I wrote inside, *For what it's worth, I love you, boobs*. I grabbed the book now, ripped out the page, threw it in the garbage. His dog in the corner watched me do this, scorned me for it, told me that I was being a bad, bad girl.

When he came out of the shower, I said, "How far are you in the book?"

He walked over to the closet, hung the towel, moved so slow I watched his entire life unfold on his back. He came over and kissed me on the forehead. This was his way of signalling me to leave.

He said, "We can't go on like this," to which I promptly responded, "Okay," and left without saying goodbye.

SOBER PARTY

Olivia was a woman of controversy and experiment. She was an artist, and for some time, we lived off her fortune. She was born with old money but had given it all up during a war of ultimatum in which she asked her mother to sober up or else. The woman could never quit. Alice was her name. She kept a handkerchief inside her bra to wipe her mouth after she was done vomiting.

Olivia had gotten into these sober parties as a new way to meet "normal women." You know the kind—broken but not finished, down on their knees but not yet weeping. Pretty but not pretty enough to be feared.

"You wouldn't understand," Oliva told me.

I was twenty-six years old and had been accused of being a bad drunk. I masturbated regularly to punish myself for the way I looked. I looked good, and I knew it. I was told I was wrong for looking this way. I had no luck with men, or with women. Had been lonely most of my drinking years. Of course, there were people who filled the void for an hour. But I was always left. There was always a wife to go home to, a career back in the States, a cat or a dog or a fish. I had a mother who was a sadistic mourner, and her sadness bored me. So I fucked a lot, and I drank a lot, and I wrote a lot of apology letters. That's how bad I was. And then one day, I crowned myself a poet.

We arrived at the sober party just past midnight, and we looked crazy together. In love or in hatred. Being with Olivia, I was terrified. She didn't terrify me. But it was what I was willing to do when I was around her, what I was capable of—that's what terrified me.

The apartment was in the Distillery District. It was all brick, all windows, all black furniture. When we walked in, Anna was standing with a bottle of water and a plate of pickles. She was the love child of an ex–porn star and an entrepreneur.

"Baby," she said to Olivia, "what took you so long? I want you to meet Mila."

I looked at Anna, and she looked back at me. She had long red hair with streaks of pink, a pinched nose, thin lips. She took Olivia away and I stood there. There was a loose rabbit. He hopped around and nibbled at my feet for a minute.

The party was just the same as any other party, except no one was on any drug or had consumed any alcohol in the twenty-four hours leading up to that night, and none would be served. There were women who dressed to make political statements in fuck-me pumps with pencil skirts and turtlenecks, women who were modest but had a suggestive way of speaking, women who just didn't give a damn but could stay up 'til four or five in the morning. Some women were playing beer pong with soda water; others were taking body shots with water and slices of lemon. In the powder room, women were snorting crushed cubes of sugar.

"Come in," one said. "Here, we'll draw you one."

I went in to taste the sugar.

"Brown sugar or white sugar?" a woman said to me, passing a tightly rolled five-dollar bill.

"Which stands for what?"

"Brown for heroin, white for blow."

"You don't snort heroin."

"Oh, honey," the woman answered, "you can snort anything."

Someone else said, "Amen to that," so I snorted the brown sugar.

The same woman opened her mouth. It was a large mouth. It opened up like the lens of a camera. She paused before she spoke. "My husband took the boys fishing—I stayed home and drank all night. I wanted to join them. I got my keys, got in my car, turned it on, and then I fell asleep. They found me just in time."

"Excellent!" I said, and snorted another line. It was difficult to take. Hard and irritating. I crunched my face tightly together, pulling my muscles into a squint.

"Yeah?" someone else said. "I turned my house into a brothel one time."

"For me, it was when ..." a raspy voice began, and I had to get out.

Everywhere I went, women offered themselves to me. They moved around each other so quickly that it felt the same as being high. I caught a glimpse of my face on a shiny gold plate that looked expensive. "When was the last time you were sober, you bitch?" I said to the plate. When the plate didn't answer, I picked it up and threw it at the wall. The crowd went, "Opa!" and I heard Anna say, "Now we're really getting started."

I was surrounded by women who had been destroyed by their own imprisonment.

I went out on the balcony and a woman told me it was a smoke-free zone. She gave me a lollipop and told me to suck on it. She watched me for some time, but once she saw there wasn't any light left in me, she ran back with the others.

The Toronto skyline looked miraculous. I grew heavy from looking at it, dizzy and disoriented. By the time I went back into the loft, it was nearly empty. Olivia and Anna had formed a circle in the living room and lit an assortment of candles on the coffee table. In the centre there was an open bottle of bourbon.

Anna said, "We're channelling. Come, come along."

I joined them on the floor but found it was difficult to sit cross-legged in my tight jeans, which I wore when I wanted Olivia to notice me. So I took them off.

Anna liked what I had done. She got out of her turquoise dress. Her body was weak, all bones. Olivia followed.

"The problem is that people think addiction belongs to, like, old people on the street," Anna began. "If more of my friends heard me when I said, 'I need help please,' then maybe I wouldn't have gotten where I did. But, honestly, it means so much that you guys came tonight."

In that moment, I remembered another party where it was all-hands-on-Anna. There had been about four guys throwing her around like a doll, and she was laughing and singing. Her ass would get smacked by someone, and her dress would get pulled up a bit more. At one point, she took her shirt off and asked, "Who's next?" and everybody pretended not to know what that meant. It wasn't until her sister showed up and kicked everyone out that it stopped. There was a collective sigh of relief.

Olivia and I had walked home that night with nothing to say to each other. Before we got to the apartment, I puked on the sidewalk. Olivia just watched me. She was the perfect bystander. But who was I? Normally, Olivia and I would share the bed, but she locked herself in her room and I didn't see her for a few days.

In the morning I knocked on her door, I made her breakfast, I called out for her, but she wouldn't come out. I left knowing that whatever she was feeling, I was feeling it too. I had only met Anna that night. She was the kind of person you'd look at and say, "Okay, no matter how fucked up I get, I can't get Annafucked." Then I heard from Olivia that she had disappeared. Nobody knew what had happened, but it was all making sense to me now.

Now, looking at Olivia, I could tell that the tears in her eyes were tears of joy, as if she were remembering what I was remembering, and she too could feel the relief. Olivia and Anna were holding hands, and I felt like I was interrupting.

Anna kept saying in a high-pitched voice, "Inhale, inhale, inhale."

Olivia did.

Outside, rain began to pour. That was my cue to go. I stood up straight. I tried to get inside my pants, but they wouldn't fit. I decided to forget the pants. Anna closed the bottle with a look of pure accomplishment. Nobody drank. Nobody fought. And nobody died.

On Queen Street, I went into the first bar I saw, all wet and smelly and depressed. I ordered whatever was on special, and I stared at it. A thought came to mind: *I miss my mother*. I drank and drank and drank.

TILAPIA FISH

In the kitchen, my mother is dressing big pieces of blue tilapia fish, which she says was imported directly from the Congo River. It's late in the afternoon, and I am thinking of one thing most specifically. How many men have I made this exact meal for? How many women? How many friends, lovers, acquaintances? How many people who had other people, and why?

I watch absentmindedly as she beats each piece on the stomach, guts it with a small silver spoon, and flips it over and over again in a pool of oil, salt, pepper, and lime juice, sometimes rubbing her palm flat on the fish for added penetration. She used this technique on me, when I was small, moaning with growing pains in my legs, and later did the same for my father when life got the best of him.

We lived in a shelter on Victoria Park, Mother, Junior, and I, for a few months after we first arrived in Canada, experiencing our first winter. I would have been five or six, and my mother was still thin and soft. This was before she began to lose her hair from the cold. We did not have cold temperatures like this back home. We had forest fires, communal ovens for cornbread, outdoor churches, street killings. But the cold, the snow, frostbite—these were foreign to my mother. Every word, every thought, every feeling would be hidden in her pores, and when she began to faint because of low blood pressure, it would be in the way her face hardened that we could predict a fall.

In the afternoon, she'd sit in the common area, taking notes on the television programs. They were mostly infomercials and the occasional soap opera.

She repeated every new English word she heard. Sometimes, in her sleep she would say, "We," or "Buy" or "Here." She slept on the bottom bunk by herself, and Junior and I took the top bunk in the rectangular bedroom we shared. It had a small nightstand facing a window. It was through that window that we saw our first snowfall.

When she struggled to remember where we were, where the snow was coming from, what country and in which year the turbulence began, she would say in a rising voice, "We," while looking out that very window. Then, sombre, she would say, "Buy." Then, calm, "Here," repeating the words in no particular order, until there was a terrible silence in the room. It was what she knew, what she understood: here, we, buy. Words that meant: mother, immigrant, fighter. She would take her children and hold them tight to her breast, take time kissing them each on the forehead, repeating, "Buy, here, we." And when my father would come visit us at the shelter, before we could afford to all move into the townhome in the small, tight housing complex on Galloway Road, again she'd say, "Here, buy, we," sometimes peacefully, sometimes sadly. With the flat of her palm, she would rub my father's cheek, penetrating.

We don't talk about this today.

Instead, my mother asks me to come home for Sunday dinner. She tells me that I must wrap my hair when I sleep, that posture is important, that I do not need to bleach my skin, that salt and pepper are necessities.

"Chin up, stand tall," my mother says.

I listen very carefully to the humming of the fish, sizzling in the pan, saying: "Here, we, buy."

ACKNOWLEDGMENTS

All of the love to Vivek Shraya, for the tremendous support, and for being particularly incredible. Special thanks to the team at Arsenal: Brian, Cynara, and Shirarose.

Oliver McPartlin is responsible for this book design and cover, thank you.

My dear friends Laini Taylor, Ashley Magee, Olivia Mikalajunas, and Chanel Chahine for being the source of my sanity.

A special thanks to the Chahine family for providing me with shelter and dinners during the writing of this book.

Gratitude for my readers/editors/friends: Victoria Mbabazi, Chelsea La Vecchia, Leanne Simpson, Natasha Ramoutar, Adrian de Leon, Nick Lyons, Alexander Lyons, Emma Witkowski, and everyone in the creative writing department at the University of Toronto Scarborough. Many of you have read the first few (many) versions of these stories. I appreciate you so very much.

Thank you to past roommates, Metty and Lu, who've borne the writing process, which involved crying and complaining simultaneously. I owe a lot of thanks to my mentors and advisors Daniel Tysdal and Andrew Westoll.

The title of this book was yelled at me in the bathroom of a bar by Emma Halsall. I was very upset. Thank you.

Love to my siblings, and Mom and Dad.

photo: Sandro Pehar

TEA MUTONJI is an award-winning poet and writer. Born in Congo-Kinshasa, she now lives and writes in Scarborough, Ontario, where she was named emerging writer of the year (2017) by the Ontario Book Publishers Organization.

VS. Books was founded by artist Vivek Shraya in 2017 to create more intergenerational dialogue and support for artists of colour. Each year, Vivek offers a mentorship opportunity for a young writer between the ages of eighteen and twenty-four living in Canada who is Indigenous, Black, or a person of colour, as well as a publishing contract with Arsenal Pulp Press under the VS. Books imprint.

vsbooks.ca

@vsbooksimprint